# Murder by Invitation

### The first Judith Spears Mystery

## Sam Oman

MURDER BY INVITATION

THE FIRST JUDITH SPEARS MYSTERY

Copyright © 2023 - Sam Oman

Cover art: Wilkes Design

# Contents

| | |
|---|---|
| Chapter 1 | 1 |
| Chapter 2 | 3 |
| Chapter 3 | 12 |
| Chapter 4 | 16 |
| Chapter 5 | 21 |
| Chapter 6 | 29 |
| Chapter 7 | 35 |
| Chapter 8 | 42 |
| Chapter 9 | 50 |
| Chapter 10 | 57 |
| Chapter 11 | 62 |
| Chapter 12 | 70 |
| Chapter 13 | 78 |
| Chapter 14 | 84 |
| Chapter 15 | 94 |
| Chapter 16 | 100 |
| Chapter 17 | 107 |
| Chapter 18 | 113 |
| Chapter 19 | 120 |
| Chapter 20 | 126 |
| Chapter 21 | 133 |
| Chapter 22 | 140 |
| Chapter 23 | 149 |
| Chapter 24 | 155 |
| Chapter 25 | 161 |
| Chapter 26 | 169 |
| Chapter 27 | 175 |
| Chapter 28 | 184 |
| Chapter 29 | 193 |
| Chapter 30 | 202 |

Chapter 31                                    207
Chapter 32                                    212
Chapter 33                                    233

Also by Sam Oman                              243

*For my Family*

# Chapter One

## 1

Checklists are wonderful things. There are all sorts of checklist templates for, well, practically *everything*. House-work, packing for holidays, maintaining cars, and even organising the kitchen so it's always neat and tidy. But after a thorough search online, it appeared there was a gap in the market.

There is no checklist for murder.

Now the obvious problem about that was, leaving behind a checklist added another layer of incriminating evidence lying around for the authorities to bumble across. Ironically, minimising incriminating evidence was near the very top of this murder list. It was right above scrubbing the internet browser cache of the 'how to get away with murder' searches. That was a particularly silly thing to do, but alcohol had been imbibed in copious amounts, and that turned gossamer wisps of common sense into turgid keyboard punching nonsense. Many were the victims of a late-night binge on Amazon or eBay, the results of which would turn up in the mail days later with the unexpected arrival of a DVD box set, a box of toffee hammers, or perhaps as a second-hand hot-air balloon plus puncture kit.

Examining the range of murderous activities provided a surprisingly sparse selection. A good old knife in the back, or the less repellent method of a bullet from a distance, preferably fired from a gun rather than haphazardly chucked, were perennial favourites. Strangulation, suffocation, and the like were far too physical for a lazy person. An 'accident' or hit and run was far to hit-or-miss. Too much could go wrong, as illustrated by Messrs Tom and Jerry, or that Roadrunner and Coyote. More or less, everything else was just a derivation of those methods. A killer remix if you like. All except poisoning. From exotic cocktails, weird and wild herbs, to using air bubbles to stop the heart and collapse a person into a pile of limbs wrapped in clothing.

They all had their cons and pros. Mainly cons for the perpetrator *and* the victim, which wasn't ideal. So what to do? How would one commit the ultimate sin, aside from putting pineapple on pizza, obviously, and get away with murder? Well, for a start, making it look as if somebody else was guilty would be an idea. A patsy. A fall guy or girl. A Lee Harvey Oswald. Another thought is making it seem as if it wasn't a murder. That would be perfect. But if you could do that, then everybody would be doing it.

But perhaps they are? How would we know?

Maybe that's the point. Maybe they have cracked the code for getting away with murder?

# Chapter Two

2

Little Pickton was the sort of village that belonged on a quintessential British postcard. The beige Cotswold brickwork of cottages and terraced dwellings pushed so far up against the meandering roads that only the pluckiest motorists dared pass one another by, fearing they'd end up in somebody's sitting room. The manicured public lawns became the battlefields for ruthless village *floraphiles* who wage war for recognition in the next Chelsea Flower show or Britain in Bloom award.

Except Little Pickton was then carefully and prudently deleted from such postcards, so that word of such an idyllic paradise didn't travel far. Occasionally the outside world poked its nose in, with television program makers showing what city folk could buy in the country, acres of land in return for their London garden shed, were usually cast out with metaphorical pitchforks by the locals so they could maintain the tranquillity.

Little Pickton also managed to get away with the fact it was more of a town than village. It even had its own train station, although actual trains tended to be option extras most days. It was the base for a renovated steam train run by local fans. The peeping whistle could occasionally be heard across the town like the wail of a baby banshee, signalling change lay ahead.

All in all, it was a place that nurtured old secrets and welcomed new ones without so much as a knowing nod and a wink. If it had a reputation, which it didn't, it would be the place that people came to shield themselves from the rest of the hurly-burly of the Great United British Kingdom.

And it was the place that Judith Spears had called home for the last four years.

At 56, Judith had settled into the life of an early retiree. Well, that sounded better than somebody who had no desire for a proper job. She never tired of telling people she'd had enough of *those* in her lifetime. And if folks were foolish enough to linger around, she'd crack her conversational knuckles and start wandering into the grey and dreary realms of working in the Big Smoke's financial heart land. People would glaze over as they heard the words 'Canary Wharf' loom on the conversational horizon. It would be a wise person who quickly derailed the conversation onto Mrs Patterson's begonias, especially this year when some pranksters took their life in their hands and planted a few extra bulbs on the display next to the war memorial park that blossomed into a rather detailed phallic display. Local kids were the primary suspects, but the rather astute mix of coloured bulbs added a fleshy realism to the display that indicated a more skilled hand was to blame. Head ringleader of the Neighbourhood Watch and the gangrenous green fingered dictator of the town's gardening committee, Mrs Patterson, had tried to remove the offending blooms, but the local vicar had thought the display was a rather charming representation of harvest season and didn't seem to think it odd that the aubergine featured so prominently.

Judith was convinced the culprit was Charlie Walker, the 60-something ex-postmaster turned professional dog walker with his *Charlie Walker Walks* business. What his grievance with Mrs Patterson was, Judith had wasted no time thinking about, but she was sure he had plenty of motives.

That was Judith. She studied people. A skill she had perfected long ago in her career. Watch, study, learn. As a result, she had naturally integrated herself in the community by volunteering for jamborees, church fates, jubilee celebrations, stopping short of joining the parish council and the Stalin-esque Neighbourhood watch, even when they pleaded with her to take part. She was a natural problem solver. The sort of person people turned to when they were in a spot of trouble.

"Are you absolutely sure about this?" Judith asked, as she peered over the brim of her teacup with the intensity of a big game hunter.

The recipient of her stare, Maggie Tawia, looked at the letter that lay on the table between them and grimly nodded her head.

"Certain." Her slight Gambian accent added a weight of certainty. When she really got loquacious, Judith could see why she was the star of the church choir with her unique tenor.

Judith gently placed her cup down and tapped the letter for emphasis.

"It could get tricky. There may be repercussions."

Maggie finally met her unblinking gaze and nodded again. "This has been going on for far too long. I have been lied to. Cheated. Made to feel inadequate. Money taken off me. For what? For what?" She emphasised each point by stabbing the table with her finger, causing the tea in Judith's cup to quiver.

Judith gave her a small half smile and slid the letter towards herself. She carefully folded it up and slipped it into the inside pocket of her quilted Berghaus jacket. A remnant from when she used to hike for exercise.

"Then I will do it. Is he still at your house?"

"Another hour, he said." The note of desperation was unmistakable. "He was digging up the front lawn!"

Judith stood and took her retracted brolly from the table. She glanced around the empty room, and noticed somebody had put up a new noticed warning of a noisy firework show, right next to the one about the missing cat who had in fact not been missing for the last five months, but the tearoom had liked the cute feline mugshot so had left it up. Sometimes she wondered if time stood still in the village, broken by only moments of busybodiness. She indicated the teapot, but Maggie raised her hand.

"It's on me. And the scone too," she added, her eyes flickering to the crumbs on a plate and an empty miniature strawberry jam pot.

From a distance, a stranger may have thought Judith was a middle-aged contract killer, ready to club her victim to death. While not strictly true, there were many philosophical similarities.

"If he doesn't deliver," Judith warned, "then he may end up buried in that hole he's digging." With that, she smartly left the tearoom without looking back.

The owner of *Tea For Time* glanced up from behind the counter. Timothy had run the place since time immemorial and was seldom seen beyond the walls. Maggie caught his questioning gaze.

"A BT engineer," Maggie said. "They haven't been delivering the speeds they promised."

Timothy sucked in air between his teeth.

"Poor sod," he muttered. "He doesn't know what he's in for. The entire village keeps getting wiped out every time it rains. Give him a shove from me, too."

Maggie nodded in agreement. Setting Judith on him was a weapon of last resort.


"Now, see here," said Judith, wagging a finger with such vigour it was nothing more than a hypnotic blur that drew the BT engineer's full focus, like a cat chasing a red dot. "My client has a legally binding contract with your company for a guaranteed broadband speed. What you are in fact delivering is quality that makes every call to her daughter in Gambia look like an episode of Wallace and Gromit."

Employing great force, the engineer dragged his attention away from the safety of the finger and tried to match Judith's steely gaze.

"Look, love, I'm just an engineer they chucked out in the middle of nowhere to check this junction box." He gestured to an open green cabinet that the roadside hedge had almost consumed with brambles sporting small blackberries, making it more edible than mechanical. The rusting doors were open, and the electronic guts had spilled out in a mass of wiring. Judith was disappointed not to see a blinking light or spinning globe on a digital screen. "She'll have to call up the call centre to complain."

Judith, who was repressing the urge to throttle the man after he called her *'love,'* held up Maggie's letter in a bold *fait accompli* gesture. The engineer slid his small rectangular reading glasses, the sort cheaply bought in pharmacy, Judith noted, from the top of his head onto the tip of his nose. He squinted.

"That's just a bog-standard letter saying they'll look into it. They're automatically generated. I bet a human hasn't set eyes on that until your client read it."

"No, my dear boy," Judith snapped in retribution for *'love,'* although the man wasn't much younger than herself, "this is a legally binding shifting of blame from the company to you, their pawn. May I remind you, under subsection-sixty-three of the new communications act of England and Wales, field engineers must, *prima facie*, ensure services are delivered to contractual specification, as the government has made very clear in the 2014 Public Services Act, section twelve-B, or they will solely bear the consequences, especially when said client is dealing with national security issues."

Bewildered by the barrage of legalese which he wasn't sure made sense - and which Judith was sure she's cribbed from a diet of daytime TV consumer advice and crime shows - the engineer removed his glasses in the hope his sudden headache would disappear.

"Who are you again?"

Judith quickly folded the letter away and shook her head. "GCHQ is not at liberty to divulge that information. And I really do sympathise with you, stuck out here in all weathers, but you must understand your manager is the one who laid the legal ramifications at your feet. Call him if you need confirmation."

The engineer, who was still kneeling on a padded mat since Judith had pulled up in her grubby red Renault Cleo and started berating him even before she had opened the car door, chewed his tongue, and pondered. Querying why his manager was passing the buck was a fruitless task. Of course he was. That was the role of useless middle-management. While he had thought Judith was some dotty woman, there was something about the defiant tilt of her head that suggested she'd had a lifetime of ordering people around. And this entire area was the home of various government HQs, an airbase, and goodness knew what else, all hidden in the heart of the countryside. He drew in a long, slow breath.

"The problem is, I'm running the wiring here and it all checks out." He tapped the cabinet. "This is where the village's entire internet comes in." He pointed down the road, from the direction Judith had come. "And fibre-optics take it the rest of the way. The problem there are the lines don't follow the main road. They cut across this estate." He jerked a thumb over the hedge. "And that's private. The owner won't let us access the box on his land."

Judith nodded in understanding. "Ah, I see. Beacons-field. That's Terry Hardman's estate." She caught the engineer's eyes light up at the mention of the name.

Terry Hardman was, against her better judgement, the local celebrity resident. The entire area was a refuge for the rich and shameless, but Hardman was the name that residents were most sick of hearing. A TV presenter, columnist, and social media voice. In his calmer moments, he was a

9

controversial figure. The rest of the time he was a divisive one. That he wouldn't want anybody on his land was not surprising. It also meant that the fault lay beyond his house because she bet his broadband was working just fine.

"The bloke's a legend!" the engineer said with admiration. "But he's a sod when it comes to letting Joe Public look at his box."

Judith peered thoughtfully in the direction of the sprawling farm estate Hardman had bought three years ago. On an almost bi-monthly basis, he'd wound the villagers up the wrong way. From explosions on his property that cracked residents' windows, to driving unwieldy supercars through the village's narrow streets and getting so stuck that traffic was brought to a halt for an entire bank holiday three-day weekend, Hardman never stopped to think of others. That was what made him popular to the public, and generally hated throughout Little Pickton.

Judith had never met the man and vehemently disagreed with his politics, but she had a soft spot for audacity and was well aware that the facade people presented to the world was often a fragile pantomime mask to shield them from the world. Or to conceal truths the world had no place knowing.

"Then I shall jolly well get you access."

The engineer's face lit up. "You know Terry Hardman?"

"Of course. I know the whole family." Judith had heard Hardman recently shared his home with his ailing father, and that his younger brother had moved in to help. She'd seen him drift through the village, issuing embarrassed apologies for sharing his DNA with his notorious sibling. "I'll sort it out, don't you worry."

"Will... will I get to meet him?"

Judith's stern lines dissolved into the most beatific smile.

"My dear *hurffminim*." *Harry? Herbert? Herschel?* She'd mumbled his name because she hadn't caught it on the way into her verbal assault and didn't want to lose momentum by asking him to repeat it. "Of course. He loves meeting fans."

She asked for the engineer's phone number, hoping he'd repeat his name – which he didn't – and returned to her car wondering how she was going to bluster her way into Terry Hardman's highly secured estate. But bluster was Judith's ammunition. And she'd just remembered something that would give her a perfect inception point into Terry Hardman's life.

Plus, she'd always wanted an excuse to nose around the grounds and she wasn't one to let opportunities slide.

# Chapter Three

3

"No! No! No!"

The voice carried across the grounds like a guttural battle tank. A sonic arsenal that cut across the loudest room. Spoken with a timbre that warned the alpha male had arrived, and you better listen because every misguided word, loaded syllable, and controversial consonant needed to be heeded. It was delivered at a volume that proved the speaker was correct, with no need for tiresome facts. And it was instantly recognised across the country, and most of the English-speaking world.

Terry Hardman was six-foot-three and enjoyed towering over the plebs. His hair formed tight curls of brown that undoubtably came from a bottle. Either that, or they were remnants of some bizarre drunken pubic hair transplant, as a few of the nastier gossip magazines had speculated. An untucked, crumpled white Ralph Lauren shirt hung from his broad shoulders like a potato sack over his faded blue denim Levi's.

The dozen catering staff from *Wayne's Foodz*, in their tight black polo tops, form-fitting black trousers, and white tennis shoes – all looking like perfect clones – froze from repositioning trestle tables for the third time and looked at the bellowing man, anticipating yet another change of plan. They were used to hearing his warbling tones on the television. There it was funny, when he was shouting at cooks in the kitchen, and feeble-minded travel companions as he insulted his way around the globe, but in real life it sounded menacing.

"I said ten yards over there!" Hardman stabbed a finger towards the shadow of the house that was steadily creeping across the lawn as night beckoned.

"But that will mean some guests won't see the fireworks because the house is in the way," said a plump young man wearing a baseball cap. A pot-smoking smiley face t-shirt peeked from beneath his anorak. He was the DJ and impromptu fireworks organiser. He gestured across the party area. "And it's closer to the speakers, so—"

"With my father's hearing, he'd have to be closer to the bloody things!" Hardman snapped. He circled a finger to encompass the large gazebo and six tables and bellowed to the crowd at large. "Move this lot now!"

It would be the third such move since they'd arrived, and the staff were already at breaking point even before the party started. They had arrived in the belief it would be a fun celeb-filled evening, but it was rapidly turning into a miserable experience and worse, it was a *family* party. The assumption being that there would be others just as miser-able as Terry Hardman. Hardman poked Gary Mercer in the chest.

"Just make sure the music's loud and the fireworks are so violent they'll give me a suntan." He clapped his hands with a distinctive triple-clap that he'd made famous on a plethora of programs. "You only have two hours! It's imperative that this party goes with a bang!"

Terry Hardman turned his back on the staff and squinted against the autumnal sun which at that moment was peeking over the steeple sloped roof of Beaconsfield Manor, resplen-dent with lush swirls of moss and cracked slates. He'd bought it on a whim, a drunken whim, but he'd always fancied owning a farm. Not to do any of the work, of course, but to have the sprawling estate to enjoy the pleasures landed gentry did. Such as shooting things. It was a far cry from growing up in Birmingham. Except the shooting things, part.

He caught movement in the top third-floor window. Was it his father? The gnarled old patriarch from whom he'd inherited all his negative traits, and who had made growing up so bitterly lonely? Or it could be his younger brother, Stephen, a man so soaked in jealousy and bitterness you could bottle it. *Eau de Amertume*. He'd longed for a sister. Not Rebecca, of course, who was his actual sister, but a proper one who was likeable and pleasant.

Whoever it was, they quickly returned to the inner sanctum of the house. Terry massaged his right temple as migraine surged through it. He felt hot and flushed, and dreaded to think how high his blood pressure was soaring. Since getting fired from ITV for a few jokey comments about a much beloved musician and their tireless charity work – which confirmed in his mind that people no longer possessed a sense of humour but had instead inherited a hive mind of intolerance - Terry had other TV networks question his value. It was the usual blip, of course. A dose of woke political correctness before normal service could resume, but it still smarted. Or, in the case of his head, thrummed.

Add his family to the mix and stress didn't stop.

Terry Hardman stalked towards his black Range Rover. The top-of-the-line model, of course. He'd find no peace in the house, and what was the point in having an estate if he could drive to some lonesome point and chain-smoke? He had such a place in mind. A bucolic spot he could take his mind off things for a short while.

He hoped the party tonight would fix a few critical issues. It was long overdue, so the organisation had to be perfect. It had to run like clockwork, so he couldn't afford any kamikaze spanners in the machine...

# Chapter Four

# 4

"Just look as if you're supposed to be here," Judith said out of the corner of her mouth. She smiled and nodded at the giant standing at the gate ahead like a Gothic monolith.

"I don't know why you made me come," Maggie said through gritted teeth.

She was still trying to adjust the passenger seat to give her more leg room, but the lever between her legs refused to move beyond one click. Judith had always said that her Cleo was in rude health, and by rude she meant the exhaust pipe sounded like a drawn-out fart and the engine was heard to issue almost human-like expletives at traffic lights. Maggie suspected they were made by Judith herself, but lacked any actual proof.

"This mission is for you, remember? I could have been at

home, curled up in front of Michael Macintyre, instead of doing this," said Judith with complete ignorance of mid-week prime time television listings or the state of modern quality comedy. "It'll be fun. Besides, when was the last time you went to a party?"

With an arthritic squeal from the brakes, they stopped next to the giant man at the gate dressed in tweeds, muddy boots, and a traditional flat cap. But his size, pale complexion, and overall demeanour telegraphed to Judith that he was no estate groundsman, but a professional security guard. She'd seen the same sort hovering around politicians at public events, always standing out from the crowd so the security people could easily identify one another should things go awry. He was also wearing expensive Ray Ban aviator sunglasses, although it was an hour from sunset and the sky was graded with pale clouds.

"Evening, mam."

"Judith Spears." It wasn't an introduction it was a rebuttal. *Mam* was up there with *love*.

Her sharp tone put the man off his stride. "Do you have an invitation?"

"Invitation?" Judith snapped with such anger that Maggie flinched in her seat. "From my wastrel nephew, or my drunken brother?" The man's jaw moved as he tried to formulate the correct response. Judith was a master of the back foot and intended to keep him on it. "Either way, I didn't know they gave invitations to mops and buckets!" She jerked a finger to the back seat, which was crammed with mops, buckets, bottles of bleach and a range of surface cleaners. Anything she could put together from her kitchen cupboards, Maggie's terrace house, and the tearoom before Timothy had time to barricade the door when he saw her coming. Judith's scowl deepened. "Better yet, you fetch them up to the house and help clean up tonight's vomit. That's what they really think of family."

She opened her door and tried to get out so she could tilt the driver's seat forward, but the guard placed a hasty palm at the top of the door's sill to stop her. She clearly wasn't the press and didn't fit the profile of a hardcore Hardman fan, and the thought of hauling buckets for some cantankerous old aunt was beyond his job description. Plus a new cherry-red mini was pulling up behind them and the Cleo was blocking the gate.

"That's OK, mam," he said, gesturing Judith should move on.

Judith gave a deliberately long, exasperated sigh and yanked the door closed with a defiant clunk. Then she drove slowly forward, the tyres rattling over a cattle grid and causing the cleaning implements in the rear to jangle to the floor. The noise barely masked Maggie's explosive release of a breath she'd been holding.

"I never thought we'd get away with that!" she blurted with giddy excitement. She was already craning towards the windscreen, anticipating what lay beyond the bend in the road ahead. "I was sure we'd get flung out."

"More than half the battle is convincing yourself that you should be there," Judith said, peering in her wing mirror, wondering who was in the mini at the gate behind them. All she could see was the bald head of the driver, leaning out to speak with the guard. "Then the rest of it usually sorts itself out if they think it's going to be more bother proving you wrong than it is simply letting you get on with things. Besides, what sort of threat would choose to look like us?"

"You were marvellous! Do you think it will be so easy

convincing Mr Hardman to let that BT engineer in here to fix everything?"

"We'll make it worth his while..." Judith was distracted as they peaked the crest of the inclined drive as it curved around a knot of old oaks to reveal an undulating manicured lawn ahead. The black ribbon of tarmac draped around a small lake, home to most of the ducks that had abandoned the village pond for a more peaceful life on the estate. Beyond stood the old manor house. The gravel driveway was already filled with a dozen or so cars. To one side, a nest of old brick buildings reminded Judith that this used to be a working farm. On the opposite side of the house, more rolling fields swept downhill to the river that crossed the land and a wild forest half a mile away that stretched beyond the reach of Hardman's territory. The flat part of the lawn closest to the house was surrounded with various trees that had once been planted in some grand design but were now looking a little wild. A large white gazebo covered trestle tables where guests were already milling. To the right of the road, a herd of fallow deer raised their heads and stared suspiciously at the Cleo.

"That's much nicer than I imagined," Maggie said in sudden hushed tones. "I imagined an overgrown horror house. I suppose in keeping with his personality." Maggie was on the fence when it came to putting the TV celeb in a box. She wasn't one to be star-struck or panicked. As long as Judith had known her, Maggie had taken everything in her stride. Until the internet went down and she fell to pieces. She'd also learned some intriguing Gambian swearwords.

"It's amazing how much you can earn by talking complete tripe and shouting at people."

"So what's the plan?"

Judith had been vague about details when she'd convinced Maggie into coming along. The truth of the matter was she didn't have a plan. Judith worked best when improvising. That had been the fundamental skill at the heart of her career. Ex-career, she supposed.

"We'll find him and get out before things kick off."

Maggie pulled a face as her head turned between the lake on one side and the grazing deer on the other.

"That would be shame. Such beautiful grounds on our doorstep, which we never get to see. And some fine catering I bet." Her eyes went wide as a thought struck her. "And free booze." She lightly slapped Judith's arm. "Why're you in such a hurry to leave?"

Judith had already spotted the catering vans, and her stomach had pleasantly grumbled in anticipation.

"Have you eaten? I haven't. Other than that scone this afternoon. And I suppose you're right. It would be silly not to stay. Turning away a couple of distant family relations would be the height of rudeness."

Maggie nodded. "Although I'm thinking rudeness is a word he knows nothing about. And I hardly think he'd be convinced I'm related to him. If Terry Hardman was any whiter, he'd be blinding me."

Judith tutted as the smooth road gave way to the gravel driveway.

"We all emerged from Africa at some point. Stop worrying about the details. Let's try to enjoy ourselves. Besides, just think how much more agreeable he'll be after a few drinks."

# Chapter Five

# 5

Judith parked next to a battered green Honda saloon. Terry Hardman had a collection of sports cars, so to her surprise, most of the vehicles were old and unremarkable. There were a couple of newer models, but nothing that screamed *here be millionaires*. She'd gleaned that the party was solely a family affair, so it made sense the rest of the clan had normal, boring, underpaid jobs. It also fitted into Hardman's character that he'd enjoy lording over his less successful family.

Judith stopped the engine and opened her door to the clatter of several cleaning products that had tumbled forward. She no longer had a need for the props, so tossed them back into the car. It took a couple of attempts to close the door, then she ignored the front door and circled around the house, towards the sounds of the garden party. Maggie followed, which is what most people normally did around Judith Spears. She had made an effort to put on a fashionable red top and jeans to at least fit in with a smart-casual vibe, but the black puffer jacket she wore over ruined the image.

Judith hadn't changed from the tan slacks she'd been wearing all day. Sensible shoes had been exchanged for sensible boots. She'd swapped her t-shirt for a light blue shirt, which was covered by a thin black thermal coat that kept her toasty and dry in all weathers. She wore a beret that she had always thought made her look arty, and not at all French. It kept her bobbed red hair out of sight, not that the once flaming red was still vivid enough to draw attention across a crowded room. Like everything else, age had tamed the lustre, but had remarkably fended off the grey-hair assault. Judith thanked her father's genes for that. She'd inherited a slightly younger vibe that shaved at least five years off her, especially if you squinted.

The noise from party shot up as they rounded the manor house. Some modern music pounded from a network of speakers, forcing the guests to talk loudly at one another while feeling they were being held hostage by Radio One. It was a chilly evening, so guests knotted around several lamp heaters that radiated golden warmth. Judith didn't break her stride as she hooked a drink from a passing waiter. A quick check revealed Maggie had missed the freebie, and therefore stood out as the only person not wielding a drink. With a quick side-step, Judith intercepted another young waiter – or was it the same one? They all looked the same in their smart uniforms – and snagged a drink for Maggie. Maggie took the glass, the soft crump of her jacket accompanying every move-ment she made and reminded Judith of the Michelin Man mascot.

Maggie looked nervously around, then scrutinised the martini glass. "What is it?"

"Tastes like alcoholic coffee."

Maggie took a sip, gave an "ooh" of delight then took another longer gulp. "Espresso Martini. Fancy!"

The alcohol vanished as it meandered through the crowd. Free food was one thing, free alcohol was worth fighting for. Judith made a mental note to pace herself. She needed Terry Hardman to be crapulous, not her. Maggie's confidence was bolstered when a tray of *hors d'oeuvres* drifted past.

"Ooh, look. It's one of those French finger *bouff-ets!*"

By the time Judith turned around, Maggie was already pursuing the food through the crowd. She drew her attention back to the guests who were slowly building in number. Some had spilled from the house, and nobody looked thrilled to be here. Even with the free food and drink on offer, it would have been a schlep to attend a Friday evening, especially as the range of accents suggested people had come from all corners. There were a few faint smiles and snatches of conversation from family members who usually only saw one another on Facebook. She eavesdropped a nearby conversation and picked up the name Gwen, then waited for the two women to part before she intercepted the aforementioned Gwen with a big smile.

"Gwen! Gosh! How long has it been? You haven't changed at all!"

Gwen's smile broadened as Judith leaned in for cheery kiss on both cheeks. The smile remained in place even though Gwen's eyes glazed over in confusion.

"Oh, thank you. Yes. No. Neither have you. How long has it been?"

Judith's hand fanned dismissively. "We'll I couldn't summon the enthusiasm to come to the last one. You know how it is."

Gwen nodded in understanding as her eyes pinballed Judith up and down, seeking a clue to her identity. "I'm only here for Robert, to be honest. I heard he'd gone downhill since his last birthday."

A brief Wikipedia search on Terry Hardman had produced a few scant details on his personal life. His mother had passed away when he was younger. Robert = father.

"Me too. Last I saw him, he wasn't looking too good."

Gwen visibly relaxed as she settled into family scandal mode. "Rebecca had moved in here just to look after him when his donepezil stopped being effective. Terry was always away working and when he was here, I reckon he couldn't be bothered. Poor thing. I heard she's cut off almost all contact with the life she had in Leeds."

"No!"

Gwen nodded. "I said packing things up was a mistake. But it does have that whiff of inheritance quackery." Her voice dropped to a whisper barely audible over the music droning from the speakers. "You know how that goes."

Artfully arranged garden lights came to life in the fading light. Judith looked up at the rapidly darkening sky and nodded sagely, although she had no clue what Gwen meant.

"Of course. Well, that's a complication I suppose."

Gwen nodded and spoke in low tones. "And Stephen, huh!"

Judith had seen the brother occasionally sulking around the village. Gwen was watching the lanky sibling enter the house through the backdoor. "He's a waste of space. I don't know why he insisted on moving here."

Judith clocked a bald man with him. The two were having a heated exchange as they entered the house.

"Oh, there's Terry!" Judith said, waving towards the house. She hadn't seen him, but it was excuse enough to follow Stephen inside the house where she assumed Terry would be. "Excuse me, Gwen. Let's catch up later."

She spotted Maggie sat at a table eating from a plate crammed with nibbles. A man in chinos, that were so tight they were anatomically accurate, leaned on the chair next to her, talking with windmilling arms. That would keep her out of mischief for a while.


The stone-flagstone corridor wasn't quite what Judith had been expecting when she entered Terry Hardman's house. She'd imagined the millionaire would have conducted some Grand Design makeover, but the floor had been worn over a couple of hundred years, back when the house was new, so the stone was now undulating. A corridor branched off deeper into the house, and a nearby open door revealed a large pantry with shelves filled with various supermarket branded cans. Mostly baked beans, canned hotdog sausages, and bags of pasta.

A uniformed Wayne's Foodz clone stepped out of the next door along, holding a tray of sausage rolls, which he lifted over Judith's head in his haste to get outside. Judith peaked into the large kitchen. It was the size of the living room in her cottage, with dark green aga on the narrowest wall, and a large old oak table dominating the room, around which several Foodzies were preparing the catering, which mostly involved reheating the foil trays they'd brought along. There was no sign of the two men. Judith took the branching corridor, guessing that the sitting room would overlook the garden and not the front of the house. The corridor cut deeper into the house and opened slightly to accommodate a narrow staircase that circled up three floors. Ahead, it ended at a partially open panelled wooden door. Light from the room beyond spilled through holes between the warped wooden slats. She could hear Terry Hardman speaking to somebody in a voice that was low for him, and normal for anybody else.

"He's got to get his arse out there and make an effort."

"He won't!" It was a woman's voice. "And this whole thing was badly thought out. Typical of you!"

"If you can't say anything nice, then don't bother."

"Well, what do you expect? If he found out..."

"He won't. Where's my bleeding phone gone?"

Judith held back near the staircase as she listened. Was it a lover's tiff? She tried to recall if Hardman was married. Recently separated or divorced rang a bell. She regretted that she hadn't kept tabs on the gossip channels, especially surrounding Little Pickton's only celeb.

"That's not going to happen," Hardman snapped. "At least not yet."

"What about the others?"

Judith braced herself, ready to run should the sitting-room door open. Now was clearly not the best time to argue her case to allow the broadband engineer to inspect a box.

"I'll sort them out," growled Hardman.

Judith tensed as she heard footsteps, then was puzzled by the obvious sound of feet on creaking wooden steps. Was there another staircase further in the room? She recalled the countless hours watching reruns of Downton Abbey. Stately homes were often a warren of servant passages and staircases. A loud bang from outside made her flinch – and made the footsteps stop.

"What the hell are they doing?" Harman bellowed.

More pops and wheezes from outside heralded the start of a firework display. The music ramped up with a disco version of happy birthday played at stadium concert levels of loudness.

"The stupid moron!" Harman fumed. "Why has he started now?"

The footsteps rapidly ascended the steps. Sounds of movement came from within the room. Judith's instinctive self-preservation warned her that Terry Hardman's quickest route out was the way she came. She quickly spun on her heels and rushed back towards the kitchen. She'd just turned into the corridor when she heard the sitting-room door squeak open. She quickened her pace and ducked into the kitchen, bowling over a waiter carrying a tray of mini burgers on buns. The food flew around her and the metal platter clanged on the stone floor as two figures rushed past without investigating the noise.

"Oh, silly me!" Judith exclaimed, catching the dazed waiter before he fell over. "Let me get a brush and help you clean this up."

Judith dashed back out, past the pantry and floor brushes, and followed Terry Hardman out into the garden.

The wall of sound that greeted her was unbearable, and she stopped in her tracks. The sky was on fire, making her wonder if the fireworks were some sort of homage to the end of the universe, or the victim of an error. Most of the guests were covering their ears from the sonic disco onslaught, while simultaneously staring into the sky with a mixture of fascination and horror.

The flash of fireworks created colourful after-images when she closed her eyes and completely spoiled her night vision, thus making it almost impossible to see where Terry Harman and the woman had gone.

Only when the music abruptly stopped, did she see Terry Harman standing at the DJ setup in the corner of the gazebo. The fireworks continued with a vengeance, each boom echoing across the estate like thunder. Then that too came to a sudden end.

Tinnitus played a merry tune in Judith's ears. People were looking in her direction, their faces drawn out in horror. Some pointed fingers. It was an odd reaction to greet a trespasser with, and for a moment she wondered if she'd stepped into a zombie film.

"I can explain," she said, lifting her hand to calm the masses.

Then she noticed they were looking just beyond and to her right. She slowly turned to see a man lying face down on the floor. He wore a dressing gown and a single slipper. But that wasn't the odd thing.

The odd thing was that his neck was broken at a sharp angle, and blood was slowly oozing from beneath him, soaking into the grass. Judith took an involuntary step back. Movement from a window on the third floor made her look up. There was nobody there, but the double full-length windows were open, and a curtain flowed in the breeze like dog's lolling tongue.

Then the screaming started.

# Chapter Six

# 6

Detective Sergeant Raymond Collins had secured his first victory of his day when a mug of PG Tips was placed before him, the perfect shade of mid-brown, with one sugar to tickle his tastebuds.

He shifted back and forth on the uncomfortable black metal chair that party guests had been using and spoke loudly over the hammering rain on the gazebo above him. The heavens had opened before he'd arrived at the crime scene, and washed the body clean of obviously incriminating evidence before a tarpaulin could be found to cover it. Forensics would be at least another two hours, so he had to make do with his Detective Constable Sarah Eastly, to take photos on her phone. The only problem with that was her artistic flare tended to take over, resulting in crime scene photos that belonged in the National Gallery.

DS Raymond Collins sipped the tea and peered at Judith over the edge of the cup. She raised her eyebrows in anticipation but didn't speak.

With a sigh, Raymond lowered the cup. "You must see how this looks, Judith."

"Absolutely, Ray. There is devilment afoot for sure. Or it was a tragic accent."

"I was referring to your presence here, more than anything. And it's Raymond. Actually, as I'm on duty, it's Detective. Sergeant. Detective Sergeant," he amended.

Judith gave a slight shrug. "And miss a party with fireworks?"

Raymond gave a dismissive snort and looked across at the rain-soaked tarpaulin and DC Eastly crouching to get a low-angle shot, with the light from the open door artfully cutting across the scene.

The best summation the detective could whip up to define his relationship with Judith was somebody he 'knew.' 'Friends' was an oxymoron. As was 'colleague' or 'associate' as they'd bumped into one another during a previous criminal incident, and Judith carried a village-wide reputation before her. The woman typically defied falling into a category, and if there was something DS Collins liked, it was neat boxes in which to file people. DC Eastly had suggested 'frenemies,' but DS Collins felt that was giving Judith too much credence.

"You found the body."

"I was standing closest to the body. I think most of the sixty-two guests found the body before I did."

"Always the last to know." Judith nodded, ignoring his

wrapped package of sarcasm. "I must say, I find it peculiar that Mr Hardman invited you or *anybody* from the village to a family party."

"We have plenty of things to discuss."

"Is he aware of them?"

"Not in so many words."

Raymond took a bigger gulp of tea as an autumnal shiver passed through him.

"How do you know the deceased?"

"We didn't have time for formal introductions, what with him being dead. I believe he is Mr Hardman's father. Mr Hardman, or Robert," she added as an afterthought. "Although I only know that because people began wailing his name."

"And he was dead before you saw him?"

"He was lying down in a pool of his own making, if that's what you mean. I dashed over to him and felt for a pulse, but to be honest, I think his broken neck was the give-away."

DS Collins circled his right hand, gesturing her to continue. "Please, elaborate. It isn't call and response. I'd like to finish this cuppa before it goes cold."

Judith focused on a point in space just above his head as she walked through the details, carefully editing them as she went on.

"I was several yards behind Mr Hardman and that woman," she wiggled her fingers absentmindedly.

"His sister, Rebecca?"

Judith filed that information away for later. "I was in the kitchen," she added for a splash of colour. "I'd accidentally knocked over a waiter, and it was raining those mini-beef burger things."

"Sliders." Raymond hated himself for adding details.

"If you say so. They were ahead of me. I stepped out to see the sky was on fire and the music deafening. I saw Terry over there," she gestured to the DJ's space, "turning everything off. Then everybody looked at me and screamed."

"You didn't hear him fall?"

"Other than a disco rendition of Have a Funky Birthday, I could hear bugger all. He was just there. A fall from an attic window, I believe. A terrible accident."

"So it would seem. Was there anybody else in the house at the time?"

"Lots of Waynes. The catering staff, she clarified."

"But everybody else was outside?"

Judith gave a dry chuckle. "I was. As for everybody else, I do not know. People could easily walk in and out as I did."

"Indeed." Raymond slurped his tea again. "And why were you in the house? Mr Hardman, the non-deceased, told me that guests were instructed to stay outside."

"As I said, I was in the kitchen in search of a glass of water, and not an Espresso Martini, hoping to catch Terry on his own."

The detective opened his mouth as another question formed, when a pimply-faced uniformed officer poked his head from the house. "Sir!" he bellowed, gesturing for attention.

"What is it?" Raymond shouted back over the increasing rain tattoo.

"The guests are getting antsy and want to go home."

Raymond huffed. The Hardman siblings had all said their father was in the early stages of dementia and prone to wandering around. The noise from the fireworks had probably drawn him to the window and over the parapet he spilled. There was nothing to suggest foul play, and no reason to keep innocent and traumatised people from heading home, especially with a colossal storm breaking and local country lanes liable to flood.

"Make sure you have everybody's details. I'll be there in a mo."

The officer nodded and ducked back inside.

DS Collins stood. "Oi, Sarah Spielberg!" DC Eastly looked up from the awkward position over the body, capturing a dramatic angle. "That's a wrap. We have to let the witnesses go."

"Oh, thank you," Judith said. She stood up.

"Not you, though. I'd like a few more details. Besides, you haven't far to go home, unlike the good people couped up in there. I'll be back."

Pulling his coat collar tight, he hurried into house with DC Eastly close behind.

Judith considered following. After all, Maggie must be inside too, sensibly keeping in the warmth. Her willpower nudged her towards the house, but her legs carried her across the gazebo to the DJ deck.

It was nothing more than a camping table with a plastic folding seat next to it. It wasn't a fancy set up. A small laptop with a virtual mixing board on-screen, and a long playlist of mostly songs from the eighties. It was connected to an amplifier, which was now turned off. Coaxial cables from the back weaved towards the network of speakers around the garden. She noted the amplifier power had been turned off by Terry. She also saw that the amplifier volume control, and every graphic equaliser dial had been tuned to maximum. It was hardly the audio wizardry she expected from a professional DJ, no matter how cheap they were.

She was about to turn away when she spotted another

laptop on the spare chair tucked under the table. The lid was fractionally open, issuing the screen glow that had attracted her attention. She knelt and lifted the screen open. A piece of software called *Firemaster* was open. It looked rather complicated, but the one message she did understand was the flashing window saying OVERRIDE.

Judith used a clean napkin on the nearest table to wipe her fingerprints from where she'd touched the computer and moved it back in place under the table. Then she hurried after DS Raymond Collins. She'd experienced a life of apparent coincidences that told her there were no such things. And Robert Hardman's trip out of the window was one of them.

# Chapter Seven

7

The large sitting room was crammed with people. Terry Hardman sat on a large sofa. To his left sat a woman in her late thirties, her brown wavy hair tied in a sloppy ponytail, her eyes red from crying. Judith assumed this was sister Rebecca. On the opposite side was Stephen. In his late forties, his thin build was folded into the curve of the sofa, his feet raised up on the cushion. His skin was pale, but there was no mistaking the resemblance to his older brother. That would be if Terry was several stone lighter and regularly worked out. In a state of shock, Stephen stared unblinkingly at the floor. Terry sat on the end of the couch, his head bowed in his hands, fingers massaging his damp hair. The guests radiated around them, putting Judith in mind of an ancient Roman amphitheatre. The two police detectives stood at the centre, with a pair of uniformed officers ushered onto a broad, curving oak staircase that wrapped around the far wall.

DS Raymond Collins was in full flow when Judith entered, squeezing between relatives like an ice breaker. He paused and gave her a black look. Judith noticed Maggie wedged in a corner shielded by a pretty redheaded woman and clutching a plate of hors d'oeuvres from which she slowly fed herself.

"As I was saying," Raymond said, turning back to the throng, "The officers at the door will double check we have all your details and we'll be in touch. If anybody would like to talk to us, please stay behind or call me any time. Losing a loved one is always tragic, and should you find yourself in need, don't hesitate to seek counselling from your local GP." He hesitated as somebody sniggered at the thought of getting a GP appointment. "Any questions?"

One woman held up a shaking hand to a chorus is fed-up sighs from her relatives.

"What exactly happened to dear Robert?"

"That is to be determined. So far, we're looking at a terrible accident."

From across the room, Judith saw Gwen frown as she looked sidelong at Terry Hardman. It was a blink-and-you'll-miss-it reaction, but it was at odds from surrounding faces.

Raymond rubbed them together, a nervous habit he had when talking to large groups. "Now the weather's turning nasty, and the roads around here are poor at best. Drive safely."

*And think yourself lucky that you're not being breathalysed*, thought Judith as she remembered them swarming on the cocktails.

The two uniformed officers shunted through the crowd and exited through a far door that led to a spacious entrance hall. The crowd silently filed out like reprimanded school children, leaving their contact details as they did so. Maggie motioned towards the door, but stopped when she noticed Judith hadn't made a move. She was watching the detectives move closer to the three Hardmans on the sofa and talk quietly. After several moments, Terry suddenly glanced up and spotted Judith.

"And just who the hell are you?" he said, standing sharply.

Judith glanced around to double check she was the object of his anger.

Terry looked at DS Collins and Judith. "I thought she was with catering, but it appears we have a gatecrasher."

"I assure you; your gates are intact. I'm Judith Spears, and my condolences to you all."

"You were the first to daddy's side?" Rebecca said quietly.

Judith hesitated, wondering if the meek voice was the same one that she'd heard behind the closed sitting-room door talking to Terry Hardman. She couldn't be sure.

"Yes, I was. Poor man," she added, groping for some neutral statements of fact. "There was nothing I could do. Did somebody actually see him tumble?"

"Nobody saw a thing," Rebecca said, dabbing her eyes.

"The whole bloody lot were wondering why Apocalypse Now was happening outside," Terry snarled. "And who knows who else was rambling around the house?" There was more than a hint of accusation in his tone.

Stephen spoke for the first time. "Terry..."

Terry sucked in a sharp breath and reached into his tight

jeans pocket to retrieve a squashed packet of cigarettes and a green lighter. It took a couple of clicks to get a flame, and he dragged heavily on the cigarette, ignoring the cough from DS Collins who edged away from the smoke plume forming around the TV host. The nicotine seemed to calm him a little, but his hand was shaking.

"I know I should be vaping," he muttered.

"Perhaps you should talk to the DJ about that," said Judith. "I mean the audio-video assault, not your nicotine habit. Wasn't he the one controlling of the display?"

Stephen shot his older brother a look. "Cutting corners again? You said it'd be a professional company."

"Don't start," Terry hissed. He poked a finger at Judith as he addressed DS Collins. "She's right about that. The bugger wasn't at his desk when I got there. Come to think if it, I haven't seen him since."

"A lot was going on," Rebecca said quietly.

DC Eastly flicked through the pages of her notepad. "We do have a Mr Mercer who said he was in charge."

Terry waved the glowing coal of the cigarette in her direction. "That's the bugger."

"He left with the others. Said he'd send somebody to pick up his gear when forensics had finished with it."

"He cocked up the fireworks, the sound, *everything*!" Terry insisted. "In dad's state, he would have been like a cat in headlights. Confused and out of his head."

Judith nodded. "Exactly, donepezil can have that effect on a person." When Terry's face contorted with a series of frown lines, she added, "As your Aunt Gwen pointed out." She'd had chance to Google the drug and discovered its use in controlling Alzheimer's. With a simple association by name, Judith had sidestepped the fact Terry still didn't know who she was. Roll over *Derren Brown*, she thought.

"You should be hauling Mercer back here," Terry insisted.

"That's the man you employed?" Stephen said tartly.

DS Collins held up a hand to waylay the brewing family argument.

"Please. You've all been through a lot. We will be pursuing each and every line of enquiry, but for now everybody needs to take stock. We must wait for forensics to arrive, so in the meantime perhaps a nice cuppa will help everybody."

Terry paced over to the window, issuing another cloud of smoke through his nose like an angry dragon. "You know where the kitchen is."

Raymond Collins raised an eyebrow, but accepted he would be the master of his own brew.

"Good. Judith, come with me, please." He marched out of the room.

Judith fell in step behind him, and Maggie and DC Eastly followed. Judith caught Terry Hardman double-talking when he saw Maggie was in the room with them. Both Stephen and Rebecca were talking quietly together and didn't look up.

Only when they were in the kitchen did DS Collins speak again.

"So why exactly where you here?" His frown deepened when Maggie entered. "The both of you."

Maggie held up both hands to fend the question off. "I'm putting the kettle on, darlin'." She set about it, further confusing DS Collins whether she was a guest, staff, or a gatecrasher.

"Maggie is my client," Judith explained patiently.

"Client?" said DS Eastly, who was making notes in her pad.

"Yes. And you'd do best to listen to Mr Hardman about that DJ fellow. Sounds like he has something to hide."

"It sounds as like you're avoiding my question."

"I'm seeking justice for Maggie. Her broadband is awful."

Raymond Collins' mouth moved up and down a few times before he could get the words out. "Broadband?"

"Yes. He's refusing access to his box." When the detective looked bewildered, she clarified. "There is a box that needs servicing on Mr Hardman's estate, and he is refusing access to it."

DS Raymond Collins looked between Judith and DC Eastly, still searching for a piece of the story he'd misheard.

"Sugar?" Maggie interjected.

"Eh? Oh, one." DS Collins was on the back foot. "Sorry. Why are you here again?"

Maggie clattered the kettle onto the aga and set out opening cupboards in sequence as she searched for cups.

Judith gave a theatrical sigh and waved a hand in the air.

"Detective, it seems to me that the party outside was a distraction."

"One that confused the deceased?" asked DC Eastly.

Raymond Collins wagged a finger at her. "No. Don't encourage her, Eastly."

"It was a distraction for murder!" Judith said grandly.

DS Collins pinched the bridge of his nose as a headache rumbled behind his eyes. By now he should be already home and watching *Only Fools and Horses* reruns to take his mind off a dismal day. Perhaps, as a treat, he'd order a pizza from

40

the local takeaway. They weren't particularly nice pizzas, but it reminded him that the usual Asda ready meals he bought weren't as bland as he imagined.

"Judith, please bear in mind when a bunch of police officers gather it doesn't necessarily mean there's been a crime."

"We spent two days tracking down a missing cow last week," Eastly volunteered. She quickly looked away under her DS's withering gaze.

Judith bobbed on her tiptoes, a habit she still retained from her youth. "In that case, dear Detective, if there is no crime there is no reason for us to hang around. Unless the police wish to become involved in a broadband dispute? between you and me, it would be a wonderful thing to bolster the force's image. It affects the entire village."

DS Collins let out a string of unconnected syllables, which were punctuated by the piercing whistle of the kettle coming to boil.

# Chapter Eight

8

After the excitement of Terry Hardman's garden party, the subsequent two days saw a constant downpour that water-logged fields and swelled the river, which led to a handful of roads escaping Little Pickton becoming impassable, unless you had a sturdy 4x4 or a canoe.

Judith had dropped Maggie at home, promising that her broadband ordeal was far from over, then she returned to her cottage on the northern edge of the village. It sat back from the road, behind a large hedge that was almost as tall as the building itself, making it easy to miss by those not looking hard enough for the pair of light-grey brick gateposts, sans gate, that marked the short gravel driveway. Judith's first task, aside from gutting the kitchen and repainting the lounge, was to remove the stone plaque bolted to the gatepost. It was still known locally as *The Brambles*, as the two successive owners had insisted on calling it, but Judith decided to call her new home *The Unnamed*, so affixed a blank stone plaque in its place. She'd moved to Little Pickton for a quiet life, so anonymity was high on her agenda.

Of course, renaming her home with a blank name quickly became village gossip, and Judith's insertion into village life meant everybody soon knew who she was. That suited her just fine. By quickly establishing *who she was*, gossip moved on to other things, bypassing the traditional *who was she* elements.

She seldom invited people over and, as she did this weekend, she enjoyed being surrounded by trinkets from around the world, all diligently collected on her travels. It was mostly cheap tat rather than expensive mementos and antiques, but they meant something to her.

She'd recently bought a dozen jigsaws from Amazon and had managed to put two of them together before losing the will to live and abandoning the others. They'd do for prizes at the Christmas Fair. She should have paid a visit to the local supermarket to buy some fresh things for the weekend, but a combination of the rain and diligent research on Terry Hardman had whittled the hours. Days, in fact. She was just preparing to walk to the village, despite the continuing rain, when she heard the crunch of gravel outside. Peeking through the curtains, she saw a dirty blue BMW saloon pulling up next to the little Koi pond, with its bubbling waterfall that was the centrepiece of her front garden. DS Raymond Collins was at the wheel. She watched him check his hair in the rear-view mirror, smoothing it down before he got out. Judging by the age and state of the car, she surmised that it had been a gift to himself to help cope with a midlife crisis.

She opened the door just as he was reaching for the camera-cum-doorbell. He flinched in surprised.

"Ah, Judith. Good morning."

"Good morning, Detective. Or is it Raymond today?"

Rain plinked across the cars in the driveway. When Judith offered nothing more, Raymond nodded inside.

"Raymond. May I come in?"

"Why? Is it important?"

"Well, it's important that I don't wet. I don't want another cold."

"I was on my way out to the shops."

"Oh."

"So you'll need to be quick." She opened the door wider so he could enter.

In the short time he'd been standing outside, his jacket was dripping wet, and his hair flattened. Pools of water formed at his feet. Luckily, the terracotta tiled floor could cope with it.

"Kitchen," Judith instructed.

Raymond followed her finger and couldn't resist nosing around the living room, which was filled with bookshelves, her laptop, television, and an assortment of magazines. Souvenirs clung to every inch of shelf space. By almost walking into him, Judith marshalled the detective into the kitchen. He looked surprised to find it was ultra-modern, with integrated cupboards and a hob that blended with the black marble worktops.

"I didn't know you were a cook."

"There's a lot you don't know about me." She almost

added that included she couldn't cook to save her life but had been meaning to practise.

"Coffee?"

"A tea if you have it."

She selected two mugs from a cup stand and switched the hot water dispenser.

"So, what brings you here? Have you solved my broadband conundrum?"

He was about to remind her that wasn't a police matter, but instead watched as she spooned instant coffee into a pair of mugs as the steaming water trickled noisily out. He waited until she had made both cups and sat down at the kitchen table before speaking again.

"Thank you. My favourite type of tea."

"With one sugar. I remember from my waitress duties the other night."

"Maggie made the brew. Anyway, that's what brings me here."

"Was her tea that good?"

"What made you suggest there had been foul play over Robert Hardman's death?"

"My magical sixth sense."

"May I remind you, keeping information from the police is a serious offence."

"Oh, so you're 'detective' today? And this is suddenly a serious case now? Perhaps a case of the *told-you-sos?* I'm intrigued."

Raymond Collins had strategized how he would wheedle information out of Judith, but she had just knocked his plan aside.

"The coroner's report came in this morning, and I stress that what I am about to tell you is confidential, but it seems there are many questions surrounding Robert Hardman's death."

"If it's so confidential, then why are you telling me?"

Good question. In the occasional encounters he'd had with Judith Spears, he'd come to know that she possessed skills that shouldn't be overlooked.

"Think of it as so confidential that Terry Hardman has sued people for less libellous things."

"Then I shan't write it down. Unless you meant slanderous?"

"I shall ignore the pedantry."

"I was being didactic. Although, I confess that now I'm being pedantic." She blew her coffee to cool it down.

Raymond sucked in a long breath. It was already a long day, and it wasn't yet eleven o'clock.

"There was a high concentration of levodopa in his system. Still within acceptable levels, but perhaps not concurrent to the level of his condition."

"Was that his Alzheimer's treatment?"

"He was diagnosed with Parkinson's, not Alzheimer's. There are some overlapping ailments, and levodopa is used in both."

Over the weekend, Judith's online research had already revealed this, but she wanted to see just how much DS Collins was willing to impart. She's spent an afternoon reading articles about Parkinson's disease. Depressing medical pieces she'd normally avoid. Amongst them, she'd located a story from two years ago regarding Terry Hardman's father being diagnosed. When you're as famous as Terry, the rest of the family is not defined by names, just their relationship to him. She wondered why Gwen had misdiagnosed her own brother. She'd also noted the side effects of the drug.

"That can affect balance. Make him dizzy. And with the loud music and fireworks, well, he may have been startled."

"Indeed. Leading to a terrible accident."

"But..."

"But there were slight contusions on his wrists, as if somebody had held them tightly. And another on his back, between his shoulder blades."

"The perfect spot to give somebody a nudge."

Raymond nodded and slurped his coffee as he watched Judith process the information.

"Well, you have plenty of witnesses."

"When asked on the night, nobody saw a thing. So what would you do?"

"Me? Why ask me?"

DS Raymond Collins couldn't help but smile. "Why not? I looked you up. You appear to have an intriguing history."

"I don't have a history, detective."

"Which is exactly what I find intriguing."

Judith's nail tapped the side of the cup as she regarded him thoughtfully.

"The most obvious thing to do is to find out who was in the house when he fell."

"Now there's the thing. That's like herding cats, except far less cooperative. I have seventy-two potential suspects who all vouch for one another."

"Maggie was outside. And a woman called Gwen."

"Gwen Meadows. Terry's aunt."

"That's her."

"And there was you."

"I was in the kitchen. I would also add the minor detail that you should look at people who have a motive."

DS Collins rubbed the throbbing vein on his temple. "Thank you that, Judith. I think that's the first lesson they teach us in Detective School."

"Right after spelling you name and badge number correctly. What I meant was, it's perhaps best to look at things from another angle."

"Such as?"

"Who wasn't there?"

"That is a long list. I wasn't there."

"I mean, who wasn't where they were supposed to be?"

"You mean the DJ bloke?" He thought for a moment. "Gary Mercer."

"That's the fellow. Or should that be *felon*?"

The detective couldn't stop his eyebrows from twitching. "Yes, we shall be speaking to him to get his version of events, and—"

"I would like to be there when you do."

DS Collins leaned back in his seat. "Judith, this is an active investigation—"

"But not yet a murder enquiry?"

"Well, no, but..."

"Then I don't see any reason for you to refuse."

"Aside from the fact this is a police matter, and you are as much a suspect as anybody else?"

"I was in the house, as the waiter I bumped into will attest to. Terry and his... well, a woman, were also in the house."

"His sister?"

"I didn't see her face. I only heard her talking."

"About what?"

Judith feigned she had trouble recalling. Raymond gave a dry chuckle.

"You're forgetting I know you have remarkable recall, Judith."

"I think they were talking about Mr Hardman deceased. About him being stubborn and that things having to change."

"Witnesses say Terry was outside at the time. He was the one who stopped the music."

"True. But that depends when his father fell. Had we exited the house and strolled straight past the body? I doubt I would have heard him fall because the music was so loud. However, they were in front of me, so couldn't have nudged anybody through an attic window. Do you have a precise time of death?" The detective shook his head. "I see. And no witnesses who saw him fall?" Another shake of the head. "As I said, I'm pretty sure he wasn't there on my way into the house, but that still leaves a three- or four-minute window before I came back out. During which time, the fireworks went off and Terry marched outside. And wasn't it he who organised the entire event?"

"Are you suggesting that he could still be responsible?"

"Not at all! Aside that such a public claimed would automatically paint you and your investigation in a poor light, draw the attention of the world's press to your doorstep so that every move you made would be analysed and criticised... it such speculation would be slanderous." She tapped her finger on the cup again. "But it's a rather intriguing notion, isn't it?"

# Chapter Nine

# 9

Gary Mercer lived just over thirty miles from Little Pickton, in the suburbs of the city, which was still considered *local* by Little Pickton standards, especially if you wanted to see a film at the cinema on a screen bigger that your own television.

Gary lived in a block of flats that once would have been a no-go area but was now in the midst of gentrification. There was even a new fresh falafel eatery opposite the entrance. The area was on the up, as was Gary's flat on the fifth floor which boasted both heating and double glazing.

Judith and DS Collins sat on a threadbare Ikea sofa, which had a name like *blotcharse*. Mixing desks, speakers and other sound equipment filled every available space. The kitchen was full of takeout containers balanced on the rubbish bin, and a sideboard had his wallet, keys, comb, small tub of hair gel, and a small Hugo Boss aftershave bottle which suggested that he occasionally tried to make personal groom effort. Gary sat on a tall bar chair, peering down at them like an Emperor Penguin.

"When will I get my gear back? I have another event to cover next week."

"Hopefully not too long," Collins muttered vaguely. "When we wrap things up. We're just filling in a few details. Who hired you for the event?"

He paused to think. "That would be Teza."

"Teza?"

"Terry Hardman."

"You're friends?"

"Not exactly. But we got on, like. Especially when I offered to drop me price."

"Why would you do that? The man's rich."

Gary shrugged. "I wanted the gig. Looks great on the socials. DJing for Terry Hardman."

Judith leaned over to Collins who was making notes in his pad. "He means *social media*."

The detective's pen gave an irritated pause before it continued scribbling across the paper.

"And you were responsible for the firework display too?"

"Ah, well. Sort of." Gary shuffled him his seat, his ample stomach poking through the gap between his jeans and frayed red polo shirt, his belly button peering at Judith like a cyclops. "His original bloke couldn't make it, but he'd already bought all the fireworks. I had a mate who had the control software."

"Firemaster," said Judith, causing DS Collins to look at her in surprise.

Gary nodded enthusiastically. "Yeah. It's dead easy. It has a ton of pre-sets and you just set the times. It shows you what's gonna happen on the screen."

"So the apocalypse theme was intentional?" Judith asked, before DS Collins could open his mouth.

"No. It should've lasted four minutes. A slow build that looked cool. He wanted a bit of old school Jean-Michel Jarre. Something went wrong. I darted off to see what'd happened."

"Couldn't you have just stopped the computer?"

Gary shook his head. "It had an error message and wouldn't do nothing."

"It had been overridden?" said Judith, ignoring the side-long look she received from the detective. Gary nodded. "Why did you start early? Didn't Mr Hardman have a set time in mind?"

"Supposed to be seven, but he was late. He was supposed to text me, but I didn't get one. I went looking for him, then it all went pear-shaped." He scratched his nose. "I'm not being funny, but can we wrap this up? I've got a shift at the hospital."

"Oh, you're a doctor," Collins said straight-faced.

Gary shook his head. "An orderly. Got to pay the bills until the music starts paying."

"Of course. Any idea why he would tell you to start before the party got really going?"

Gary shrugged and slipped his phone back in his pocket.


"Curious," Judith said as they drove back to Little Pickton.

"Curious about what he said, or curious that I let you convince me to come along?" Raymond Collins said as he pulled onto an A-road.

"I don't mind being your fall-girl. You need a buffer if you're going down the slippery path of accusing a celebrity of a crime."

Collins wasn't so sure, but Judith had sounded convincing when they were in her cottage.

"That doesn't mean you get to ask the questions."

"Then you shouldn't dither so much."

Raymond's indignant silence was broken only by the thrum of the wheels on the road. Raymond reached for the radio but stopped when Judith spoke up again.

"Why didn't you bring that delightful young detective constable with you?"

"Eastly? She's behind a desk, making calls and chasing down leads."

"Impressive. She's a confident young woman. Did I detect a frisson between the two of you?"

Raymond looked at her so sharply that he veered his BMW into the other lane, only jerking it back as a car in his blind spot honked its horn.

"That's wholly inappropriate!" he barked.

"I mean she's a pretty thing, and you're a successful man with a chiselled jaw and a midlife crisis." She patted the dashboard.

"I meant because she is a colleague and I'm her superior. And I'm old enough to be her father. Well. If I'd started early…"

"I'm just making conversation. I've been told that I'm a good judge of character. Goodness knows why you're unmarried. Unless you're a secret serial killer, or this irritable façade isn't really a front."

"You know nothing about me."

"I thought we were getting to know one another."

DS Collins attempted to reply, but couldn't manage it. Instead, he bit his lip and tried again.

"How do you know about Firemaster?"

Judith looked nonchalantly through the window. "I thought that was obvious? If Gary isn't as inept as he presents, then it sounds like sabotage, doesn't it?"

"Has anybody ever told you that you're a very overly dramatic person?"

"What do you know about the brother and sister?"

"Stephen and Rebecca? Very little."

"Stephen has made a fine career as a failed actor and a failed entrepreneur. He never got on with his brother, they always argued, and he saw himself as constantly passed over when it came to opportunities."

"How do you know this?"

"I spent my weekend researching our case."

"There was no case until this morning. In fact, there still isn't one. And there is no 'our' in this equation. What we're doing is pure due diligence."

"I like to plan ahead. His sister is another matter. There's less in the papers about her."

"I know DC Eastly will be delving into–"

"She was an English teacher at an Academy in Leeds. She turned it in to look after her father. At some point, Terry suggested they both come and live at Beaconsfield, so she quit her life there and move down here. She was engaged, but that fell apart and since moving she's lost touch with the friends she had there. One escaped to London, and she often thought about moving there. I think her life is one of regret." She gazed longingly at the traffic ahead. "One of hampered dreams. Not that she has grand ones like her brothers. She wanted a regular life and a cat." She gave a drawn-out sigh. "And her poor cat died before she moved away. She's been carrying a chip on her shoulder, and now she has nobody else to blame for the way the rest of her life shapes out."

It took several long seconds before she realised Raymond Collins was throwing her looks in between trying to keep his eyes on the road.

"What?" she said innocently. "People like posting their nonsense on Facebook. It's often what is unsaid that speaks volumes. And there was a great deal unsaid."

"What about Stephen?"

"He had a fling with Twitter. Mostly political nonsense. Nosing where he thought public opinion lay rather than any genuine hard and fast beliefs. I bet he was considering going into politics, but he didn't manage to be entertaining or controversial enough to get many followers, unlike his brother. Another fail there."

Raymond puffed his cheeks. He was impressed, but was loath to show it. He and DC Eastly had spent the weekend looking into the family, just in case, but had drawn only a thin profile. The only chunk of research they had was Terry Hardman's police file. It consisted of some accusations of bullying from his ex-wife, which were settled out of court. He'd lost a dozen libel cases, had numerous parking fines, and had a suspended six-month sentence for assaulting a TV producer when he'd been fired from a hosting a game show.

"Anything about their father?"

"Lost his wife twelve years ago and never recovered from that. The Big C, the poor dear. Raymond worked as a handyman most of his life. When Terry made some money, there were rumours he'd borrowed cash some for various business interests, but nothing successful. I found two ventures that still had websites registered to him, but they hadn't been updated for years."

Once again, DS Collins remained silent. That was a shed load more information than he or Eastly had uncovered. He thought back to the first time he'd met Judith Spears and reminded himself to do what he'd set out to do then, dig a little deeper...

# Chapter Ten

# 1°

With most of the day missed and over with, and conscious there still wasn't a scrap of food in the cupboards, Judith asked DS Collins to drop her off at the village green. They said a pleasant goodbye, or rather a cordial one, as the last hour had been terse small talk in which Raymond dodged questions about his personal life. He countered with less than subtle probing questions about Judith pre-Little Pickton, which she enjoyed frustrating him by dancing around the answers.

It was still raining heavily, and she hadn't brought a brolly, but her coat had a sensible hood which kept her dry enough to dart into the local Budgens to get provisions. Due more to the weather than the time, the store was quite empty, so Judith got the groceries she needed within minutes. She made small talk with Beth at the checkout, who confirmed that the incident on Hardman's estate was still very much the gossip currency of the day, then she was on her way, briskly walking home clutching two biodegradable plastic bags filled to bursting point. She was convinced the rain was actively degrading the bags with every step and doubted they would make it intact to her cottage.

Two cars passed her in the main street, and somebody with a black umbrella quickly made their way past on the opposite side of the street. Other than that, she was alone with her thoughts and the skittering rain as she made her way up the gentle hill to the T-junction and turned left towards home.

Which made it all the easier to notice the car following her. Especially because her stalker was making a ham of it.

It wasn't particularly dark, but enough to warrant turning on the headlights, which made it conspicuous that the driver hadn't. It was an electric vehicle, so deathly quiet as it moved a few dozen yards, then stopped. Then rolled forward again, like an inept cat stalking a mouse.

Finally, because of the rain, its brakes gave a long, low squeal every time it stopped. After the fifth stealthy squeak, Judith stopped in her tracks. Rolled her eyes. Then slowly turned around to face the car.

It was a hundred yards behind her, stopped at the bus stop. The wipers brushed the rain aside, and she saw the silhouette of the driver, who must have noticed she was staring because they made a half-hearted attempt to crouch below the dashboard.

Judith raised a shopping bad in clumsy wave. The occupant's panic increased, and, to her surprise, the car began to slowly reverse back the way it had come. The driver did not try to speed up. It was just a drawn-out retreat, as if they hoped Judith wouldn't notice what was going on. It overshot the junction leading down the hill to Budgens. Stopped, and then gently pulled forward, rolling down the hill with just a whisper from the tyres on wet tarmac.

Fifteen minutes later and she was home just as the rain seeped through her jacket. She considered calling DS Collins to report it, but thought better of it. After all, nothing had really happened. Not yet, any way.

When DS Collins didn't contact her the following day, the thrill Judith had been experiencing, that she was part of the investigation, soon ebbed. Being a witness wasn't much fun if you had witnessed nothing to begin with. She may have been the first to reach the body and overheard a rambling conversation that suggested both Terry and Rebecca Hardman were innocent when it came to shoving the old man out of the window, but it was all moot and of no use to anybody. To compound matters, Maggie had called her to complain that her broadband was still on the blink. Judith felt a twinge of regret for offering to help, but knew she'd be mortified if she hadn't done so. She tried to be tactful when telling her perhaps now wasn't the time to bring up access to a junction box to a man who'd just lost his father.

Still, it was an itch that she couldn't quite scratch and there were too many niggling threads regarding the night of Richard Harman's death. That she hadn't been entirely open with DS Collins was also irksome. Some things were best left unsaid, but when it came to possible murder, tactful silence wasn't the best option.

She made herself a tea and considered redoing a thousand-piece jigsaw of *A Sunday Afternoon on the Island of La Grande Jatte*, which she'd completed so regularly she no longer required the picture on the box for reference. In fact, she'd finished the jigsaw so many times that it felt like a penance to do it, but that was the point. If Judith wasn't busy, she became anxious, worried that she was frittering her life away, and Georges Seurat's pointillist masterpiece was as good an analogy for this as any.

She even ventured back into the living room to take the box down from the tall bookcase it was perched on when she caught sight of a black envelope on the doormat in the hall. The motion detector on the front door should have alerted her unless that battery had depleted, although that was unlikely.

She peeked out of the front window, but it was now too dark to see beyond the thin pool of light spilling from the window and across the koi pond. Moving into the hall, Judith stooped to pick the envelope up. It was black paper, with no markings or writing on it. She turned the hall light on and opened the front door, shedding light across her Clio and down the otherwise empty driveway.

It was raining harder and there wasn't a soul around.

Checking the Ring doorbell revealed somebody had covered the camera with mud. It would have meant entering the front garden though another route and edging around the house sideways, so they were not detected. It was a lot of effort when they could have simply pulled on a hood and kept their head bowed to remain anonymous.

She cleared the mud from the camera and hurried back into the house. She angled the envelope in the light in case there were any clues etched on the paper, but there was nothing.

The water from the hot water dispenser was still filling her cup when she slipped a finger in the corner of the envelope flap and slit it open.

# Chapter Eleven

1 ¹

"I don't know how to work this bloody thing."

"I think you pop it in there and give a good yank," Judith suggested.

"You don't see George Clooney having a problem sticking it in the hole."

"Let me."

Judith nudged him aside and took the small capsule. A quick check showed it could only go into the hole in the machine one way. She dropped it in, then pushed the silver lever to trap the capsule inside like some Medieval torture device. With a choice of a whole two buttons, she selected the one showing the largest cup. Second later the Nespresso machine whirled to life, dribbling scalding hot coffee into a waiting cup.

"I thought these posh coffee makers could do a lot more." She looked between the cup and Terry Hardman, who was leaning against his kitchen table, arms folded defensively across his chest. He wore a dark blue lumberjack shirt, with the sleeves rolled up to his elbows exposing hairy arms, and jeans that were far too tight for his – and Judith's – comfort. The bags under his eyes looked darker than ever, and Judith wondered if he'd slept since she'd last seen him.

"I got it as a freebie at some awards event." He shrugged, as if that explained everything.

"You get free coffee machines?" Judith was impressed.

Terry indicated around the kitchen. "I didn't have to buy half the junk in this house. There's an inverse rule of thumb. The more famous you become, the less you have to spend on crap."

"Well, if you ever need to get rid of some of this junk..." Judith said leadingly.

"We'll discuss your fee later," Terry said, thudding the conversation back to the matter at hand. Judith filed the word *fee* away for further examination.

"Your letter was unexpected and ambiguous."

Judith had extracted a single white postcard from the envelope with a message scrawled in small block-caps in black pen:

## 8PM - BEACONSFIELD MANOR

Terry gently scratched his forearms, more out of a distraction than need. "To be honest, I wasn't sure what to do. I've hired private dicks before." He glanced sidelong and clocked Judith's frown. "When ex-wives start carping on about excessive divorce settlements and the odd crazy woman claims we're having an affair."

"I read that really happened."

Terry held his hands up *mea culpa*. "Well, *that* one was real, but you get some crazy birds and some who like to take advantage..."

"And you'd rather *that* not get in the newspapers."

Terry cocked a finger at her in a silent '*exactly!*'

As the Nespresso finished gurgling, Judith handed the cup to Terry.

"You don't get much in a mug, do you?"

He added a splash of UHT milk from a small plastic carton on the kitchen table. "I bet Clooney gets commission on each capsule. That's why he's minted."

Judith made another cup for herself, then followed Terry into the sitting room. He didn't say a word as plonked himself on the sofa, where he'd sat when she'd last seen him, and pulled out a cigarette. Preoccupied, he rolled the cigarette between his fingers and watched the unlit tip bob up and down.

Judith circled the room, for the first time taking in the luxuriously thick carpet and modern fittings that blended into an old-style stately home. There were half a dozen speakers sunk into the ceiling, spread out between the recessed lighting. At first glance, what looked like antique cupboards turned out to be deliberately worn modern fittings, and there was a television the size of a swimming pool mounted on the wall. There appeared to be some ingenious mechanism holding it in place that moved it back into the wall. Several framed pictures showed Terry in exotic places, often with his co-hosts from his various shows. There was a conspicuous lack of other family members.

She turned around just as Terry put the cigarette back in the packet and slumped back on the sofa with a wheezy sigh.

"I should really pack up. Maybe start vaping. Isn't that what all the kids do these days?"

"I couldn't say."

Terry finally looked up as if registering Judith's presence for the first time.

"So I heard you're something of a private sleuth."

*Ah*, thought Judith. *Let's see where this is going.*

Terry continued. "I asked around. Well, not me, obviously. I got people to ask people."

Judith nodded. "Six degrees of separation."

"And you're something of a secret weapon."

"Am I? Well, an amateur sleuth, perhaps. I may have found a few cats and dogs in the village."

Terry's brow lowered, his caterpillar eyebrows almost concealing his eyes. "However you want to play it. But I know you've been consulting with DS Collins on what happened."

Judith sat down on an armchair opposite and held her coffee mug with both hands. For all the wealth on display, Terry Hardman was certainly frugal when it came to keeping the heating on. Evidently, Mr Mercer had been in touch after they'd left. Perhaps innocently asking when his much-needed gear would be returned. Perhaps. Judith just gave him one of her trademark easy smiles. One laced with subtly that radiated a confidence that she knew what she was doing. That wasn't strictly true, but it was better than constantly correcting people's misconceptions.

"My deepest sympathies to you and your family."

Terry's head bobbed in a manner that suggested he didn't require platitudes right now.

"Obviously, the press ran with the story today." Judith nodded knowingly, although she hadn't thought to check a single paper all day. "And it's just a matter of time before they spin 'accident' to something dirtier."

Judith sipped her coffee. She wasn't sure how much DS Collins had shared with Terry Hardman. Probably nothing if this thing turned into a full murder investigation.

Terry didn't register her silence. "And that's when things will get uncomfortable. If I went to proper private dick, and word got out... well, how do you think that'd look to the paps?"

"So what is it you require of me?" asked Judith, ignoring the word *proper*.

Terry shifted in his seat. His eyes darted to the doors and staircase before he spoke. This time his voice was low, and Judith wondered how many other people were in the house.

"Find out who did it."

Judith tensed, but her smile remained in place.

"So you think it was murder?" Terry's eyes darted around the room, and he shrugged. "Have you shared this with the police?"

"Do you think I'm soft? Of course not. I need to be ahead of the game on this – if it's true, of course. *If* this... *when* this gets out, how do you think it will affect my career?"

He huffed, as if the apocalyptic answer was obvious. The man had just lost his father and all he could think about was the impact on his career. Was he so callous, or even a sociopath? Or was there something more?

"Who do you think would do such a thing?"

Terry raised both hands to the side in an expansive gesture. "Who wouldn't? Apart from me, obviously."

"Obviously."

Terry's eyes shot to the staircase as he spoke. "Stephen's too fragile to handle accusations like that. And too temperamental. Dad made a career of pissing the family off. We were poles apart."

Judith tried to imagine the opposite of Terry Hardman. All that came to mind was a docile Giant Panda, which wasn't much help. She let him carry on.

"He was vile to pretty much everybody. I mean, over the last two years, his Parkinson's had got worse, and his mind wasn't lucid. More often than not he started forgetting who I was. Me!"

"Unimaginable."

"Exactly. And he'd left behind a knot of... financial problems."

"Such as?"

Terry didn't blink as he met her gaze. "Private things. You know how it is. But I think there was somebody at the party who I didn't invite. Other than you..." Judith's smile broadened a little more. It was a perfect response. "Clive Wilson." He looked expectantly at Judith. "You know...?"

"Do I? Is he a footballer...?"

"He's a critic. Worked for the Daily Mail and a few other quality papers before going freelance and spreading his poison everywhere."

"Ah, not a fan then, is he?"

"I would say his ultimate achievement would be destroying me."

"But killing your father is, dare I say, I tad extreme."

Hardman gave a sharp laugh. "Him? The git hasn't got it in him. But somebody like Wilson could manipulate and frame me for murder. And he's not the only one." She could see his hands were shaking. "I think a lot of people that night would like to frame me for something I didn't do."

Judith's coffee mug froze halfway to her lips. She slowly

lowered it as the words sank in. Terry was in self-preservation mode. The loss of his father was minimal compared to his own plight.

"You believe that you're being framed for your father's death?"

Terry emphatically nodded.

"That's..." she wanted to say extreme, but stopped herself when she factored in the ego of the man sitting before her. Terry Hardman had made a multi-million-pound career through sheer personality alone. There were no unique skills he possessed, no stunning insider knowledge on any subject. She could tell he was a smart man from the few phrases he'd slipped into conversation. Perhaps he was business savvy, too. But to rise in fame based on nothing more than force of will required an equally proportionate ego. She changed conversational tack. "Why do you think you are being set up? And not your siblings?"

"Because they're nobodies," he said dismissively. "What makes a better headline? Think about it."

"And what conceivable motive would you have for patricide?"

Terry Hardman couldn't hide the gleam in his eye. It was fleeting, but Judith was certain she'd caught it, and she was pretty sure it wasn't because she'd used a fancy word.

"Now we're getting into nebulous waters." Terry leaned forward, resting his elbows on his knees. He seemed more alert, as if enjoying the intrigue he was layering. "Tell me a family that doesn't have reasons for bumping off one-another. You're going to hear a fair few, but I'm hoping you'll see them for the distractions they are."

Judith placed her coffee mug on the table and stood. She

slowly paced the room, taking in the photos on the wall. She felt Terry Hardman's eyes following her.

"So if I am to get this right, you are hiring me to find out who killed your father, if anybody, before somebody at the party is able to set you up in the official police investigation?"

"Yep. You can come and go here as much as you want. Speak to Stephen and Rebecca. That's if they'll talk to you. Talk to anyone if they'll speak to you – which I doubt. But I need results quickly. I don't know how much time I have. Oh, and I'll pay you ten grand."

Judith couldn't suppress her half-smile. It was one of disdain. Money was not a concern for her, but Terry misread it.

"Okay, twenty!"

Judith turned on her heels and held her hands behind her back as she'd seen TV detectives do so many times.

"I shall tell you what my fee is in due course. But for now, I accept the case."

Terry Hardman visibly relaxed and slouched back against the sofa. He looked genuinely relieved.

Judith couldn't help but wonder exactly *what* stories about her he'd heard.

"I'll tell you one thing that would lubricate the wheels of my investigation," she added. "I've always fancied a Nespresso machine."

# Chapter Twelve

# 1 [2]

Miss Marple never had to suffer these problems, Judith thought as she teased another Ginger Nut biscuit from the packet. When that doddering sleuth had a mystery to crack, all the suspects were conveniently in the same house, or in the worst case, village. Or at least she assumed they were. She'd read none of the books and only had fleeting memories of the many television adaptations. Judith made a mental note to broaden her reading pile and pick up a few of the classics. However, she was certain Madame Marple didn't have to jump on several trains to navigate in the most indirect way to Leeds just to interview a witness.

Aunt Gwen, or Gwen Meadows, was Richard Hard-man's sister. Or estranged sister, according to Terry. Judith recalled the woman looked in a state of shock after events, but so did most of the people gathered that night. The question was, was it *enough* of a state of shock? Judith pondered as the train pulled into the imaginatively named Leeds City station.

After visiting every coffee shop in the station to meet, but discovering that tables, chairs, or any level of comfort, hadn't quite made their way to Leeds station, Judith texted Gwen to meet at a Costa around the corner. She paid for two medium cappuccinos, that were almost the size of her face, and a tuna melt sandwich which scalded the roof of her mouth at first bite. The receipt was neatly folded away for her new client to reimburse her.

Gwen clutched her coffee with both hands as if preparing to nosedive into the froth. She wore jeans, a quilted green jacket, and a fluffy black scarf to chase away the chill. She didn't possess the air of somebody who'd just lost a brother.

"He was always difficult," Gwen said without preamble. "Since we were kids, Dick was the domineering type. A loudmouth. That's where his children get it from. Well, Terry, at least."

"So you didn't talk to him much?"

Gwen harrumphed. "Sometimes five years would pass before I heard a peep, or a Christmas card landed on the mat. Although, cards flowed a little freer when Rebecca started looking after him."

"Because of his condition?" When Gwen nodded, Judith pressed harder. "What do you think was wrong with him?"

Gwen sucked in a long breath as she considered her response. "Richard and I were the only children our parents had. We'd always had a prickly relationship. You know how kids are. When he had his family, we practically never spoke to one another. When his wife passed, I reached out, but his response was cool. He had his hands tied, bringing up those three. Why would be want somebody like me back in his life?" She slurped her drink and gazed into the middle-distance. "When my husband went, I was surprised that he turned up at the funeral. Maybe he felt as if he knew what I was going through and sympathised? The whole thing knocked me for six. I was placed on antidepressant. I still need them," she added with a thin smile.

"Anyway, we didn't talk about what had happened, but we kept in touch a little more. That's when he told me about his big fear. He thought he had Alzheimer's. Just subtle things at first, but he was terrified. It was about that time Rebecca started looking after him and he was officially diagnosed with Parkinson's. That didn't make him feel any better, and Terry's people made hay with the media. He was on daytime telly every day, talking about it. Milking it for appearance fees. Contact became less frequent. I don't know if it was him or her. Rebecca never warmed to me. I suspect she was told I was the uncaring aunt who never visited. Who knows? The few times I spent with him were warm. I felt as if there was regret that he'd pushed me away. He still wasn't convinced it was Parkinson's, and I wondered if Terry thought him inheriting Alzheimer's would somehow affect his career?" She held up a hand. "I'm just speculating on that." She lapsed into a brief silence. "I didn't get to talk to him much after that. Rebecca became his gatekeeper full time and then he moved to the estate because Terry thought he could provide better care. Well, Beaconsfield Manor is much nicer than the ex-council house he was living in." She stared into her coffee froth.

When Judith had reached out to talk to her, Gwen had

been quite amiable and hadn't inquired in what capacity Judith was poking her nose in. It was assumed that if she was willing to travel halfway across the country, then Judith must be more than a professional busybody. For her part, Judith had considered a Zoom call would have been easier, but meeting in the flesh was more useful. She knew from experience that online it was easier to bluff and hide telltale body language cues. Micro-expressions were lost in grainy video, so lies and misdirection were far easier to achieve. But even in-person, Gwen appeared unruffled and sad.

Judith rapidly circled a finger. "Let's rewind. If communication with your brother had become sparse again, then why were you at his birthday party?"

As Gwen considered the question, she rotated the cup in her hands a full three-hundred and sixty degrees before answering. When she did, her gaze followed an island of chocolate that bobbed in her cup.

"Terry had made a point of inviting everybody because I think it was clear he might not be having another. His condition was far worse than when I last saw him." The muscles in her jaws clenched, but she said no more.

"Did he invite you?"

"Who? Dick? I don't even think he knew I was there. From what I heard, I wouldn't be surprised if he knew it was his birthday."

Judith rolled an unopened sugar sleeve between her fingers. She found the gently grating of the granules inside therapeutic and it was cheaper than a fidget spinner. "So you didn't see him?"

"No. No one was allowed to before the party started."

"Who said so?"

"Stephen."

"Did he say why?"

Gwen shook her head. "I just received the invite. Me. None of the kids. I think Terry has forgotten his has cousins."

"So who sent it? Terry?"

Gwen paused again as she took a deep sip of coffee. She was deep in thought, a frown knitting across her forehead as her gaze became unfocused. Judith didn't think it was the time to draw attention to the blob of frothy milk that now adhered to the end of Gwen's nose.

"I don't rightly know. Stephen, I suppose. I mean, Terry remembers Christmas and sends the odd text, but it's not as if we're that close. And Rebecca's a right little madam. She was born without initiative, that one. That's why her mother had a Caesarean. She would've got lost on the way out."

Judith tried not to stare at Gwen's nose as the milk started to slowly coalesce and form a drip. "But if Terry was throwing the party, then why wouldn't he have invited you?"

"Good question. I suppose Terry enjoys putting his name to anything he's not involved with. It makes him look impor-tant. He's made a career out of it."

Judith quietly filed the information away. Terry Hardman exuded a confident, can-do-anything attitude, but that was evidently a cover. The fact he'd employed her because he thought he was being framed confirmed that. And Aunt Gwen's words supported his suspicions.

"So you think Stephen organised the party? Is that the sort of thing he'd normally do?"

"Ah..." Gwen didn't back that up with any verbiage. She stared into her drink, lost in thought.

"Ah...?" echoed Judith. When it was apparent Gwen wasn't willing to elaborate, Judith placed her cup onto its saucer with a little more force than necessary, snapping

Gwen from her reverie. Her eyes snapped up to meet Judith's.

"I think you're talking about the inheritance."

"Yes, I am," Judith improvised firmly, while wondering why Terry hadn't mentioned this.

"Well, rumour had it that Dick changed his just after he became ill. Bequeathing a sizeable sum to his sibling."

"That's you?"

Gwen nodded and raised her eyebrows. "You can imagine what the others were thinking."

"From a handyman who lived in a council house, I would be wondering what there was to inherit."

"Terry bought the house for him early on and I heard he'd lent him money to help his business ideas. It's not something we really got into. Needless to say, the kids got angry that, just as Dick and I were being friendly once again, this happened."

"I can imagine."

"The thing is, I was told none of this by Dick. It was Stephen who brought it up. He was furious. Said I was cutting into his inheritance."

"I take it his children would all get a share?"

Gwen shrugged. "You'd think so, but Dick was an unpredictable man. Terry is loaded, so it's not as if he needs a penny. Rebecca never had much time for her dad when she was younger. She harboured a grudge when her mum died." She dropped her voice to a whisper. "I think she was only doing the doting daughter carer routine to ingratiate herself back into his good books. Not that he had any good books." As if reading Judith's mind, Gwen sharply sat upright, tilted her head imperatively and resumed her normal volume level. "But of course this is all unsubstantiated and if my brother cast this in a will, I was never officially told by his solicitor, or is it a lawyer these days? Anyway, nobody has come knocking with news of any such windfall."

Judith smiled warmly and sipped her drink, adjusting her manner to one of supreme understanding. "Naturally. I mean, such a simple A-to-B route to inheritance would place you firmly as the number one suspect."

"Exactly." Gwen nodded, although her confidence was ruffled. She stirred her coffee, eyes glued to the foam bubbles orbiting the cup. "That is utter nonsense, of course. Anyway," she added as an afterthought. "I have an alibi." She clocked Judith's questioning look. "You. I was talking to you before you darted inside. Leaving me *outside*," she added firmly.

Judith pondered that. Gwen couldn't have entered the house without passing her, could she? Then she remembered there were two staircases. At least. Was there a third? It wouldn't be infeasible in such a grand house.

Gwen chuckled dryly. "For all I know, it was you who shoved poor Richard out of the window."

Judith forced a smile as she suddenly realised how flimsy her own alibi was with the good folks in the police. She filed that away for later scrutiny and cleared her throat.

"Just one more thing. With such family squabbling, what about the other guests at the party? Would any of them have motives to see Richard dead?"

Gwen bobbed her head side-to-side thoughtfully. "Very probably, but nothing off the top of my head. I haven't seen half of them for a good while. We're the sort of family who only convenes for weddings and funerals."

"And now, murders, apparently." Judith raised her cup in silent cheers and drained the rest of the coffee.

At that moment, Gwen's mobile rang with an unknown number. She cautiously answered to the dulcet tones of DS Collins. A quick "I'm speaking with your colleague right now" raised a frown when the good old DS wondered just who that colleague was. Judith couldn't hear that side of the conversation, but guessed as much. She patted Gwen on the arm and made a hasty departure, mumbling about needing time to dash for her train.

While on the train home, she missed several calls from DS Collins and, for once, was thankful for the poor phone service she was paying Three mobile the privilege for every month. It gave her time to think over Gwen's accusations. Clearly, there was no love towards her niece and nephews, but neither was there any obvious sorrow for losing her brother. Money could do strange things to people. More money meant people took bigger risks.

She just needed to know how much was really at stake.

# Chapter Thirteen

1<sup>3</sup>

Maggie crunched the shell of a chocolate lime with as much frustration as could be conveyed in the hushed confides of the public library. Library was a generous term for the small annex next to the post office, but it had shelves crammed with books that people could borrow, and a row of six new computers locals could access. On Thursdays, it was also the location of the Book Club, which often got boisterous and had led to physical violence on at least two occasions. One of which was most certainly Richard Osman's fault.

It was Judith's intervention that had kept the library open. The local council had voted to abolish it in the last round of spending cuts. They claimed the population was too small to warrant such an expensive service. The town had been in uproar, and Judith had taken it upon herself to have a word with the councillors in question. She told nobody what was said, but the library was quietly removed from the list of cuts and - even more remarkable - money had been found behind somebody's couch to buy the computers and the broadband connection. It had helped cement Judith's reputation as a 'doer.'

"I could be doing this at home," Maggie grumbled, "If you'd sorted my internet problem out."

"I'm working on that. But for now this is the best place to do a little snooping." Judith shivered from the chill. While she had apparently performed miracles with the library service itself, repairing the heating was beyond her powers.

"What about your place? You have heating, don't you?"

Judith had thought it wiser not to have her digital finger-prints all over the information she was seeking, but thought it best not to bog Maggie down with technicalities. The choco-late limes had been the deciding factor for Maggie. It was her Achilles' heel and, as far as she was concerned, the height of British cuisine.

She'd been cross since Judith had called on her the night before, after returning from Leeds, and asked her for a favour immediately after spending several hours being grilled by DC Sarah Eastly about why she was at the party. Appar-ently, fixing a broadband connection was not a realistic excuse for gatecrashing a celeb bash. Judith assured her that she'd have a word with the coppers. The young detective constable was probably only trying to make her mark on the case with a little more verve than was required.

Maggie tapped the screen with her green painted nail. "So I can't access Richard Hardman's tax account from here. That's private, like yours and mine." Judith tried to hide her disappointment. Maggie had worked for the HMRC for several years, specialising in fraud detection, before taking early retirement, so Judith had hoped to have a straightforward route to see just how much the deceased may have squirrelled away.

"So that's a dead end."

Maggie hummed thoughtfully. "Maybe not. I still know a few people back in the office. But for now we can circle the issue. See if there is anything that could indicate the size of Mr Hardman's pile. Like this." She tapped the screen again.

"Companies House?"

"All limited companies have to submit paperwork here, including tax details. Didn't you say he was a businessman?" She typed Richard's name into the search box and a list of businesses appeared. Several were people with the same name but from different parts of the country, but scrolling down the page soon revealed a nest of companies registered to *the* Richard Hardman. "He had a decorating business here. *Brush That Limited*." A few mouse clicks summoned up the declared earnings. Maggie let out a low whistle. "I'm in the wrong job. Or I would be if I were still working."

"One point three million pounds?" Judith's frown deepened. "What was he decorating? The Humber Bridge? What sort of painter earns that much?"

"And that was just in that year."

"When he was very ill."

"Let's go back." Another chocolate lime was masticated as Maggie went back in time with her search. "Another million the year before. And before that... a loss of earnings."

Since *Brush That Limited* had started, it had made a modest income Judith expected from a handyman. Then, a sudden windfall in two consecutive years. Another business, cryptically named *Manifest Ltd* was still running, but had declared no income for the three years it had been open. Another two businesses, one of which seemed to be a window cleaning service, all folded over previous years.

"That's a lot of money to be floating around," Judith said thoughtfully. "I suppose it could have been a gift from his son."

Maggie shook her head. "Personal gifts are taxed differently, not as part of a Limited company. Perhaps a cash injection, you know, like they do on Dragon's Den?"

"Into a painting company? Again, what are they painting with that much money?"

"In my experience, it won't be there no more. I bet the money was cleared out of the account and spent on hundreds of untraceable invoices."

"That sounds suspiciously like money laundering."

Maggie's eyes widened in surprise. "And what do you know about that?"

"I've seen enough daytime TV to get the gist." Before Maggie could say anymore, Judith pressed on. "Please ask your ex-colleagues to snoop around, although I'm doubtful that money would have landed in his current account. The question is, did it come from Terry? And where is it now?"

Detective Sergeant Raymond Collins was livid. Not least because he felt responsible for unleashing the monster called Judith Spears. For some reason, her appearing uninvited at Terry Hardman's event hadn't been much of a surprise. In the short time he'd known her, he expected her to suddenly appear at the scene of anything of interest, just like magic. Especially at the site of a murder. She seemed like the type who attracted trouble and mystery. But that was when you got to know her a little. On face value, she came across as a paragon of virtue. A help to all.

And that made Raymond uneasy.

Now she was travelling the country to interview potential suspects, which meant he'd put the mistaken idea in her head that they were working together. Why had he taken her with him to see the DJ? It had seemed a good idea at the time. But now...

"Don't you think that will be a distraction?" Sarah Eastly said from across their shared desk. She twirled a biro between her fingers in a teenage habit that helped focus her thoughts. "It's not as if we're drowning in resources."

Raymond looked up from the report he had been half-reading through unfocused eyes.

"We must cover everybody without exception."

"I know, but–"

"And everybody who was there is a suspect until we can eliminate them from our enquiries." Sarah nodded and opened her mouth to reply, but her DS ploughed on. "And, of course, you know the term 'eliminate from our enquiries' is complete balderdash."

Sarah's eyebrows popped up in an elaborate display of surprise.

"Balderdash? Is that word still used this century?"

"I use it all the time. Well, perhaps not *all* the time. Only when it seems pertinent. And in this instance, it is bloody pertinent. She is now interfering with our investigation."

Eastly issued an overly loud hum. "Is she? I mean, there is no law to stop witnesses speaking to one another."

Raymond stubbornly folded his arms. "Well, there should be."

"And as far as I can see, she is firmly in the 'couldn't have done it' camp. I mean, timing, her whereabouts, etcetera."

This time Raymond raised a quizzical eyebrow. "People your age do not say *etcetera*, unless you're the King of Siam." He chuckled but stopped when Eastly looked vaguely puzzled. He waved her unspoken question aside. "Perhaps. But I would like to know a little more about her."

Eastly drew in a light breath that turned into a sigh. "Okey-dokey." She tapped her computer screen with the pencil. "But I have drawn up my own list of possible suspects if you would like to go through that first?"

Raymond stood and pulled his coat off the back of his chair as if he was a matador.

"Later. Right now I need to jump into the centre of the storm before somebody else does."

"You're going back to the house?"

"Yes. There is the little matter with Ms Hardman I'd like to discuss."

For the first time in a long time, DS Raymond Collins had a spring in his step. It was wonderful to finally have a case to sink his intellectual fangs into. A case in which he could make a difference.

He was one step ahead.

Or so he thought.

# Chapter Fourteen

# 14

"If you could just rewind a little, Ms Hardman. I don't quite understand why your father switched from private health care to you becoming his carer."

Rebecca opened her mouth to immediately answer, but stopped herself. She subtly glanced sidelong at Judith who was sitting on a wing-backed armchair in the corner of the spacious sitting room. The gesture was not subtle enough to go unnoticed by DS Collins. He couldn't stop the groan of frustration escaping his lips.

"Ms Hardman, may I remind you that this woman is not your solicitor, your guardian, or your bleeding astrologer."

"We're both Libras, if that helps," Judith said helpfully.

Collins refused to meet her gaze. "It does not."

Rebecca shook her head. "I don't know this woman.

Other than my brother telling me she'll be in and out of here."

"If you prefer to have this conversation in private...?" Collins said hopefully.

Rebecca gave a hollow laugh. "Oh no. It's nice to be able to actually speak for once. As you can imagine, with my brothers I seldom have the opportunity." She shuffled her bottom on the chair on clasped her coffee cup with both hands, peering into the milk-less liquid as if seeking answers, forcing DS Collins to prompt her again.

"So, tell me about becoming your father's carer?"

"He was never happy with the help the social services sent around. Rough hands he said. And I was the one who always got the complaints. Terry was either off filming something or shouting at somebody, so he never really acknowledged the seriousness of daddy's complaints."

Judith piped up from across the room. "And your other brother?" She clamped her mouth shut when DS Collins shot her a look. A reprimand formed on his lips, but Rebecca pressed on before he could issue it. "Stephen always said he was in search of a problem to complain about. Daddy could be a tad bit," she mouthed the word '*opinionated.*' "Especially when it came to the," again she mouthed the word '*Polish.*'

Collins bristled. Hardman senior was clearly not the type of person he enjoyed being around, but he was professional enough to bite his tongue.

"I think it was because of the war," Rebecca added, before sipping her coffee.

"We were never at war with the Polish. We were helping them out. And your father was far too young to have fought in the war."

Judith shrugged amiably. "I don't get mixed up in politics."

"Or history, it seems," growled Collins before pressing her on the issue. "So why didn't he choose another private company?"

"He was considering it. But he knew I was somewhat cash strapped and work was unbearable." She trailed off and put her cup gently down on a side table. Both hands neatly fell onto her legs, and she inhaled deeply as she met DS Collins' eye. "I appreciate you looking into all of this, but in my view, it was a terrible accident. My father was reacting badly to his new medication, and of course Terry wanted us all to be circumspect. He was terrified about the press leaping onto such a personal story."

"I thought your brother relished media attention?"

"Not of the negative personal type. He's had too much bad publicity recently, what with his last TV show being axed and his comments on... y'know. *Her.*"

Judith hid her smile behind her teacup when she caught Collins' puzzled look.

"I think she means the celeb hoo-ha a couple of months ago." Judith's hint didn't help him. "It was all over the news." Collins shrugged. "Never mind."

Rebecca nodded vigorously. She hadn't cottoned on to the detective's ignorance. "Exactly. My brother has never been one to skirt controversy. You can't imagine how embarrassing that is for me. I'm much happier when people don't know we're related." She gave a sharp sniff before continuing. "But when the controversy hits his pocket, then it's suddenly unwelcome."

"It's surprising they haven't done so already," Collins mused.

"We had some journalists poking around this morning, but they're still treating it as an accident." She shrugged. "I suppose it's not in the family's interests to have too much dirt aired in the open. They're probably too afraid of their own affairs being flagged up."

"There's always a few skeletons in the old family closest, aren't there?" Judith asked nonchalantly before realising she had stolen the very line the detective was considering.

"Well... families are families," Rebecca muttered, her cheeks flushing ruby red.

Collins leans forward, propping his elbows on his knees in a manner he thought was urgent and pressing, but because of his gangly forearms, it made him look uncomfortable. "If your brother is so opposed to bad press, then what brought you and your father to live here?"

"Well, for one, I suppose it would look awful if he didn't offer. I mean my flat was nothing to shout about and dad lived in the same old terrace he'd done for decades."

A frown slid down Judith's brow.

"Did your father not have money? I thought he had his own business?"

"He excelled in business. Every opportunity failed spectacularly one way or another. He wasn't business savvy. Success was almost an allergy."

The detective nodded in sympathy, but Judith's mind was juggling theories and teasing connections.

"So you were living hand-to-mouth," DS Collins said with more than a hint of sympathy that betrayed his working-class roots.

Rebecca nodded. "Not a nice thing, especially when your brother is loaded."

Collins' eyebrows raised like a basset hounds. "So he took pity on you?"

"You have a high opinion of my brother's emotional maturity." Rebecca forced a thin smile.

"And what about Stephen?" Judith asked, popping the moment of companionable silence that seemed to have descended in what suddenly felt like detective and suspect flirting. "Did he have any thoughts on how to help?"

"Stephen was a bitter younger brother. He and daddy didn't often see eye-to-eye."

"I thought the younger siblings were always the favoured child?"

"Not in our family," Rebecca replied tartly. She dried up, unwilling to say more. As the silence became more pronounced, she tilted her head and looked pointedly at DS Collins. "None of us want this to drag on. It was clearly an accident. The other two may act all 'alpha'" she scornfully wagged her fingers in air parenthesis. "But they are ultimately spineless."

With nothing more to be said, DS Collins wound the conversation up and stood to leave. When Rebecca was looking elsewhere, he cocked his head at Judith issuing a clear *we need to chat* edict. But Judith was not the type to be dictated to. She rose and indicated the staircase.

"I notice this old house has an awful lot of staircases. This is the second or third I've seen."

Rebecca nodded wearily. "Four. This just leads to the first floor. The main one is in the hall," she nodded towards the door Judith had last left through. "And there are a pair of creaky old servants' staircases at either wing of the house. Not that we have servants. Just the cleaner and she hasn't been here for weeks. It all dates to Downton Abbey days. Upstairs Downstairs. That sort of thing."

DS Collins motioned to leave, but Judith held her ground.

"It occurred to me I haven't seen your father's room."

"That's a crime scene," Collins interjected.

"Well, not technically. You said yourself it probably wasn't a crime and your lab dollies have swept everything for fibres and whatnot."

Rebecca nodded. "We were told the room could be used." She looked at Judith. "You're welcome to take a look if it helps. Terry was clear you can come and go as you please."

Judith shot a tight smile in Collins' direction. "Then it would be rude not to!"

By the time they climbed the two flights of servant stairs to Richard's bedroom on the second floor, Raymond Collins was already puffing for breath. The room was nothing special, with furniture and odds and ends from other rooms standing in for any lack of design. The bed had been stripped bare, but Richard's meagre personal possessions still lay the exposed surfaces: a fancy-looking watch that bore an unidentifiable logo, a half empty bottle of a pound shop aftershave, a faded Leeds FC baseball cap, and a dog-eared Andy McNab book.

On the bedside table was a plastic tablet tub and two boxes of pills. Judith made a mental note of the *donepezil* and *memantine* prescriptions before moving to the window and tripping on a pair of slippers left in the centre of the room. DS Collins' hand shot out to catch her, but she was nimble on her feet and prevented following the same fate as Richard by propping herself against the windowsill. A pair of white wooden doors offered a double-glazed view across the back of the property and the rolling wooded countryside beyond. A pair of curved brass handles were fastened with a simple latch, and bolts at the top and bottom locked the door firmly in place. Judith jiggled the handles.

"That's quite firm."

"Maybe he'd the door open to let in some air." Rebecca remained at the door, refusing to enter the room.

"You didn't do it?" Rebecca shook her head. "The last time you were in here, do you recall if they were open?" Again, Rebecca shook her head. "And remind me, who was the last person in here?"

"I think that may have been Stephen waking him up for the party."

Judith pressed her head close to the glass and peered down. The doors opened onto a tiny Juliette balcony with the rail coming just below Judith's waist. She gave the door another experimental rattle, and it held fast. Glancing down, she noted a ratty three-by-two rug underfoot. Age had faded the white, blue, and red speckled pattern and curled up the frayed edges.

She gave a short *mmm*, then flashed a smile at Rebecca.

"All hunky-dory here."


"Mrs Spears..."

"*Ms*, technically."

She heard Raymond Collins shuffle to a stop on the gravel driveway and suck in an irritated breath. She stopped and turned and gave him a questioning raised eyebrow.

"I believe a man of your status requires acute accuracy."

Raymond's mouth see-sawed open and closed before his face twisted into a forced expression of contriteness.

"Of course. But I must inform you of the repercussions of interfering with a police investigation."

"I can imagine."

"I don't want you to imagine, *Ms* Spears. I want you to–"

"Judith. I think we're beyond formality now, Raymond."

"–I want you to comprehend," he pressed on.

Judith splayed her fingers across her chest and tilted her head nobly. "I am but a curious member of the public keen on assisting you with your inquiries."

"That doesn't entitle you to travel halfway across the country to interview the deceased's sister."

Judith transformed into the image of puzzlement that was worthy of an Olivier Award. "Doesn't it? I was merely consoling the dear woman."

"And then you turn up here–"

"I was asked to." She had caught him off-guard and couldn't hide her smile. "Terry specifically invited me. He's naturally concerned about what happened. And I think with you so kindly allowing me to interview the DJ—"

"I didn't allow that!" Raymond sharply injected but stopped when her eyebrow raised again. He was starting to resent Judith's ninja eyebrows.

"My dear detective, we all know the force is under-resourced, and I am more than happy to perform my civic duty."

DS Collins squeezed the bridge of his nose and seemed to deflate as if he's found a physical stress valve. The first few syllabubs of a counter-offensive tumbled from his lips before he sucked them back and attempted to act more affable.

"Ms... Judith. We can ill-afford to have you underfoot. Suspected murder is one thing, but finding evidence of such a crime must be solid and unbiased."

"I assure you I'm not the sort to be trampled on. And I'm certain that I'm a few steps behind you. For example, the suggestion of murder in Richard's room."

Once again, Raymond cycled through various responses before encouraging her to continue with a single nod.

"The balcony door was firmly locked from the inside. It can't accidentally blow open."

"Then it must have been open beforehand."

"Well, it wasn't. Did anybody see it? I didn't. It was rather a chilly night for an outdoor party, as I recall. People were gathering around the lamp heaters for warmth. And now with that rug."

"Exactly. A tripping hazard."

"An obvious one. Too obvious. The rug had been moved from underneath the window, as I'm sure you noticed from the pale colouration of the carpet that delineated it. It had been there for some years before being conveniently moved to the French doors."

Raymond nodded, fascinated despite himself, before stopping and composing himself back to his stern manner.

"But still..."

"And there's the inheritance question."

"What question is that?"

"Surely you've been examining motive?"

He nodded, hoping that DC Eastly had flagged something up before this busybody.

"Good." Judith flashed a smile and clammed up. She could tell the DS wanted her to continue, but his pride was preventing him. "Well, if that will be all, I'm off. I have a myriad of things to do I that are expected of young retirees." She walked towards her car.

"*Mrs* to *Ms*. Divorced?"

Judith stopped in her tracks. Her shoulders rearranged themselves before she slowly turned, smile still held in place.

"My divorce was the happiest time of my life, let me tell you."

"The only record I found seems a little murky when it comes to your maiden name."

"Really? How peculiar." She shrugged. "It wasn't my first wedding, alas, so the paperwork may be dense. Am I to take it I'm part of your investigation too?"

"Until we can eliminate you from our enquiries. Standard procedure."

"Of course. Then, as a potential suspect I shall confine myself in the pool of other potential suspects, as you request."

"That's not what I meant," Raymond said sharply. He hated that she was twisting his words. "I was just wondering why records of your past are vague."

Judith rolled her eyes. "The perils of being born pre-computerization. I had to get my birth certificate for my passport once. That was such a palaver! Let me assure you, detective, I'm an open book."

She gave a cheery wave with her car keys and continued towards her Cleo. DS Collins watched her, wondering exactly *what* book she had in mind.

# Chapter Fifteen

# 1 5

Stephen Hardman walked the streets with the impunity of somebody who wouldn't be recognised even if he had his name emblazoned across his chest in flashing neon. Even his close relatives would struggle for the first few seconds, too.

Judith followed several yards behind. Her jacket's hood up against the fine drizzle, and hands stuffed in her pockets for warmth. She was currently feigning interest in the window of a charity shop, while keeping half-an-eye on her target.

So far, Stephen had driven to the local co-op and parked there without entering the supermarket. His light jacket was completely unsuitable for the weather, yet he determinedly continued to the post office. With every other step, he kept checking his iPhone held in a vice-like grip. Judith kept several people between her and Stephen, just far enough so she could eavesdrop in the queue. No mean feat, as the two elderly ladies between them were talking at the top of their lungs about the colour of 'their Barry's jumper.' Judith was sure there was much more depth to their conversation, but her focus was on Stephen. He shoved a wad of twenty-pound notes under the counter window and asked for them to be exchanged for U.S. dollars. The cashier, a woman Judith knew didn't live in the village, explained that they didn't have enough currency in stock, and she was more than happy to order it if he could wait five days. That seemed to present an issue for Stephen, who haggled the time down to no more than two days. After another testy back-and-forth, it was finally agreed that Stephen could wait five days and it would be available *sometime in the afternoon.*

Throughout the exchange, Stephen's mobile phone was balanced face-up on the counter where he could spot any incoming messages, but it remained blank. He then stalked down the street, eyeing every passer-by with suspicion, and the hope that they'd recognise him so he could justify that suspicion. But nobody gave him a second glance. He'd lived on the Estate for the past four months, but despite being the brother of a media whore, he'd somehow remained incognito. Remarkably, the media had yet to fully seize on the story of their father's death — something that had set Judith's alarm bells ringing. While gossip was the lifeblood of Little Pickton, the town had no desire to host a media circus, and none of the wider Hardman family appeared to be seeking to benefit from the tragedy. Was this because they sought privacy or were hoping to benefit from a yet undeclared inheritance?

Or was there something else? Was the family fearful of

the obnoxious, but well paying, celebrity amongst their ranks?

Observing Stephen's meandering path up and down the high street informed Judith that Stephen was burning time, waiting for a call he didn't - or couldn't - take at home. Odd for a man who had apparently kept himself to himself. Was that a conscious decision because he was caring for his father? Judith doubted it, based on his narcissistic desire to be recognised.

He suddenly stopped outside the butchers, forcing Judith to overtake him. She cursed herself for not paying attention. Keeping her distance allowed her full coverage of his antics, but now he was behind her, she was blind. She passed within inches as he looked at his phone again. She was close enough now to see he was thumbing through a list, but she was unable to make out any of the entries. If he had looked at her, he hadn't recognised her.

It was imperative that she once again repositioned behind him, so Judith quickly crossed the street, all the while keeping an eye on Stephen's reflection in the window of a darkened estate agent. She had just stepped back onto the kerb when he answered his phone, bowing his head in a sign this was a very private call. She cursed herself for rushing. Had she delayed, then she may have been able to overhear. Now, watching him take several steps one way, then the other, she could only speculate. But one's body movements were a language in themselves, and one of which she had dabbled in the many lives of Judith Spears.

First came the straightening of the back as Stephen received disagreeable news. Even though he was speaking on the phone, it was the natural impulse to make oneself look taller and more threatening. Then his free left hand gesticulated, chopping the air to emphasise his points. Whatever they were. His voice rose, audible even across the street, if not actually coherent. His ire was bubbling away, accumulating with gestures back the way he had come, towards the house, before he stabbed the screen to hang up.

While the detail was lacking, the subtext was more than ample. Stephen was planning a hasty and secretive departure from Little Pickton, and somebody had just let him down, situations had changed, or somebody had betrayed him.

Whatever it was, Stephen Hardman had just shot to the top of Judith's suspect list.

Judith prided herself on having a sensitive nose when it came to sniffing out irregularities and trouble, so she was annoyed with herself for letting the most obvious suspect slip her attention: Clive Wilson, the freelance journalist who may have been at the party.

Since arriving back at her cottage, she had assembled a timeline of events in her mind. She had cleared the kitchen table to provide a visual aide memoir using items from around the kitchen. The first, a tin of beans, represented the party invitations going out. Next to it was an onion, which she regarded as the multi-layered motivations of the Hardman family. That was surrounded by several grapes who represented the police, Mercer, the DJ, Aunt Gwen, and Clive Wilson. She was a great believer in visualising complicated situations, but all she now had on the table looked like the aftermath of a shopping spillage. She was now unsure which grape represented who and there was a tangerine to the side, which she was pretty sure represented something important, but she couldn't quite put her finger on what.

Terry Hardman had decided on the party and organised it. His father had substantial holdings in his private companies, the sort of money his famous son would earn. However, he hadn't used that for his own palliative care, and instead he'd employed his daughter who was on her uppers. Hardman and his sister had been downstairs when the fireworks were sabotaged, and their father fell from the window. Which left Stephen, the brother who was making plans to swiftly depart, as being alone with the deceased. And, as the younger brother, he had openly fumed about losing a substantial portion of his inheritance to his aunt. An open and shut case, surely?

She imagined this was the avenue to dear Detective Sergeant was vigorously pursuing. But that left one strand flapping in the wind, demanding to be answered. Clive Wilson. The ex-Daily Mail critic who had turned up, uninvited, to the party – yet nothing about the incident had made its way to the press, which was miraculous. So why would a journalist, who was now clinging to freelance work, even though he had once been a GP, sit on such a potentially explosive story? Particularly one who is so determined to ruin his career.

This raised two questions in her mind. Who had invited him that evening, and why was he sitting on such a juicy story that would have got him a fat fee from any newspaper?

She knew the answer was the simplest and most obvious one. Occam's razor, as the scientists called it. Clive Wilson was waiting for the right time to strike, to cause Terry

Harman maximum damage. Which, to Judith's attuned sense of mischief, indicated he knew a great deal about the roots of the murder.

# Chapter Sixteen

# 1 6

Light strobed from the rapidly moving knife blade as it transformed the onion into fine slices at tremendous speed. Judith watched at a distance, her eyes screwed tight as tears stung them. She was impressed with Stephen Hardman's culinary skills, even if he was only preparing a cheese sandwich.

"It's every man for himself here," Stephen growled as he scraped the onions into a bowl, then sprinkled a garnish over the grated cheese lying on a bed of sourdough. "If my brother had his way, we'd all starve or be forced to dine at McDonalds."

Judith had made an impromptu visit to the house. Partly because Maggie had continued to complain about her broad-band connection, but mostly because she was enjoying playing amateur sleuth and Stephen was the only sibling she had yet to talk to.

When she arrived, he claimed to have only just woken up. It was eleven in the morning, but his tousled hair cooperated that, and his crumpled clothes hinted that he'd fallen asleep fully dressed.

"Did you have professional culinary training?" she said, clutching the thimble of instant coffee that Stephen had begrudgingly made. He was irritated because the Nespresso machine had gone missing.

He nodded. "Two years in the kitchen." After a lengthy pause in which he topped the sandwich with another slice of bread, a brown slice Judith noted - what sort of cookery wizard mixed the bread? - and then slipped it into a sizzling frying pan, he added. "It was a burger van in a lay-by on the A24."

"Oh. Your own business?"

Stephen shook his head. "When you're stony broke, you take what you can. And plenty of people aren't fans of my brother, so when they find out we're related, it makes life hard. They're usually the ones in the better paid positions." He mumbled as he flipped the lightly toasted sandwich over and pressed it lightly with a spatula.

"Why did you leave?"

He deftly flipped the sandwich out of the pan and onto a wooden chopping board. With a single stroke, he cleaved the glistening sandwich in two. The cheddary guts oozing tantalisingly out.

"Why did I leave two years in a burger van in a layby? I hated it! My life was trickling away while I watched my brother travel the world on TV." He checked his temper, then indicated to the knife. "And lost a lot of blood before learning how to use these things properly." He tossed the knife into the sink. "Customers didn't seem to like my body fluids as a condiment."

"People can be picky."

Stephen took one slice and bit into it without reacting to volcanic heat in his mouth. "Why is my brother so keen on having you nosing around?" He asked with a full mouth, crumbs spitting out.

"He's concerned about his family."

Stephen harrumphed. "Bollocks. He's concerned about himself. Me and Rebecca are just collateral that can snag him bad press. That's what he's bothered about. But why you? He has a publicist who normally handles this sort of thing. Pays through the nose for her too."

"Because I'm local," Judith retorted with more authority than she felt. It was a good question, and one her ego hadn't considered querying. "And I was in the process of examining the estate because of a... broadband issue that's affecting the village." In the light of a dead father, she realised how lame that sounded, so she was surprised when Stephen's eyebrow cocked up.

"Oh. The junction box? That's on the far side of the estate. It's the most remote bit. Want me to show you?"

Judith's eyes shot to the knife in the sink, and she suddenly felt uncomfortable. A shiver ran through her as she pulled herself together and nodded.

Stephen guzzled down the second cheese toasty slice as he led her out of the house and around to the side protected by shade. A squat brown Tuatara all-terrain vehicle was parked there. It reminded Judith of a military golf cart with chunky off-road tyres. The two seats were enclosed in an open roll cage and the rear was a flatbed, caked in mud. It was parked amongst tarpaulins, rusting metal frames and other detritus found across an ailing estate. Stephen wiped his greasy fingers on his jeans as he climbed onboard. Judith followed, noting the key was already in the ignition. Soon they were bouncing across the lawn, with Judith - sans seatbelt - clinging to the steel roll cage for life.

"Do you enjoy living here?" She asked, the words coming in gasps as they left the relatively manicured lawn, passing over a cattle grid into a ploughed field.

"Stuck in the middle of nowhere? God, if I don't die of boredom, it'd be a miracle. I know I didn't have much of a life and I fully intended to have one. And it will be a fistful of civilisation for me. London, I think."

"I know it well. Expensive place though. That's why I moved out here."

"Who cares about that? Life is for the living. It's about time I enjoyed myself."

"I suppose after this tragedy, your father may have left you something to help?" Stephen snorted and looked at her sidelong. Judith pressed on. "My Aunt Maud left me two thousand pounds when I was younger. It changed my life."

A snarky single syllable laugh escaped Stephen's lips.

"That tight old git." He pulled himself together. "Well, I'd be surprised. Terry gave him all his financial advice, which is probably why he died broke."

Judith tried to study his face for any sign he was lying. A difficult task in a rocking vehicle. Stephen's tongue was working his back teeth to dislodge trapped cheese nuggets.

"I suppose all families have their conflicts. I can imagine having a brother like Terry is interesting."

Stephen didn't rise to the bait as they splashed through a

waterlogged section of field before pulling onto a stretch of rocky ground. His silence was telling enough.

Stephen pulled the ATV in a tight turn and cut the engine. "Here we are." He nodded ahead.

They parked at the bottom of a sloping rocky patch of land that bled into a fast-flowing river thirty feet wide, and the colour of the finest brown. It was obviously swollen from the recent downpours. Judith saw black scorch marks amongst the stones caused by an intense bonfire that left not much more than a few pieces of debris and scoops of charcoal. The scorched earth led to a rusting green junction box, identical to the one the BT engineer had been tinkering with. One end of the metal cabinet was charred and buckled. As Judith stepped from the vehicle, her feet sank an inch into the waterlogged ground.

"What happened here?"

"Terry had the idea of building a landing stage for his boat. A typical him. He hasn't a clue how to build sod all."

Judith surveyed the landscape. The fields all arced down to greet the river, with trees crowning the various hills. It was a well-concealed place away from prying eyes.

"Daft place to put cables."

Stephen nodded. "The river's blown its banks twice since he bought the house. Knackered up the phones for the village, but the river was only half the size before then. The new housing estate in Avesbury caused this. It's getting worse."

"And what about this?" she indicated the remains of the bonfire.

"Terry comes down here fishing. I think one of his camp-fires got out of control and damaged the box. Still works. It's the water damage that keeps shortening it. But maybe he doesn't want BT to see the damage he's caused. Might make him look bad."

It was at that point she noticed the handle of a machete poking from under Stephen's seat. His deft work in the kitchen sprung firmly to mind, and she wondered just what had been incinerated down by the river.

"Is this what you were looking for?" Stephen asked. Was his voice dripping with suspicion? Or was Judith completely misreading the situation as he moved his foot and caught the machete handle.

"Well, access for the engineer to fix this would be ideal. Might keep the village happy."

"That's Terry's call. He doesn't like people nosing on his land."

"It's hardly nosing. It's a public service that needs attending to."

"Like I said, my brother has his ways. He doesn't just let anybody on his land." Judith detected the tinge of doubt in his voice as he squinted at her. "So, as I asked, why is it he's letting you poke around? What have you got on him?"

Judith allowed the last sentence to ping around the various skill centres of her brain. Stephen's mind had instantly jumped to blackmail, an indication that Judith was either giving out the completely wrong vibes as a purveyor of the dark arts, or Terry Harman had been victim of such a thing in the past, which indicated he may have *something* to hide. She noted his foot caught the machete handle again. Was he rather unsubtly trying to intimidate her? Or was he really a master of clumsy incompetence?

She tried to take another step. The mud sucked her feet, slowing her movements. She wobbled precariously, only catching her balance at the last moment, saving herself from face-planting into the mud. She judged they were at least a mile from the house and further from a public road. Any screams would only be heard by crows in the field or the odd passing cow. It was a perfect remote spot for skulduggery. She knew also that she had stalled far too long in answering Stephen's loaded question.

Judith turned and pulled herself back into the Tautara, flashing what she hoped was a disarming smile at Stephen.

"What have any of us got on one another?" she said cryptically. She sat down, enjoying the worried silence in the driver's seat. A nerve had well and truly been struck. "Thank you for showing me this. I'll have a word with your brother. You can take me back now."

She issued the last as a command rather than a request. Stephen obliged without a word. The chucky tyres spray mud as the ATV lurched forward. Judith kept her focus straight ahead and resisted a second glance at something she had seen amongst the charcoal black firepit. Several small, glass vials, similar to the medication in Richard Hardman's room. It begged the question why somebody would have tried to dispose of them way out here?

# Chapter Seventeen

# 17

"Guv?"

"Mmm?" Detective Sergeant Raymond Collins didn't lift his eyes from the magazine's sudoku puzzle. He didn't dare. The puzzle help focus his mind and DC Eastly's tone contained all the frequencies of impending doom.

"A couple of things have come up."

"Did they indeed? Perhaps a little acid reflux?" He chuckled, but stopped as his eyes were forced to meet Eastly's stony face. He was already regretting what he might hear.

"Well, I diligently pursued the line of enquiry you instructed me to." Sarah Eastly had the gift of turning sarcasm into a regional accent of its own. "Ms. Judith Spears has a rather dull past. No flags on credit reports. No internet footprint. It's almost as if she was some normal middle-aged woman who lived life under the radar."

"That sounds suspicious," Raymond shot back with what he hoped was sharper sarcasm. "And she was married."

"Not according to the register. Not in this country least-ways. And she's never had a passport. So..."

DS Raymond leaned back in his seat, which gave a loud, over-dramatically long creak as he did so. "Deed poll?"

Sarah shook her head. "Not that I found. I didn't bother checking to be honest, because I interviewed Maggie Tawia, Gwen Meadows, and the security guard hired for the event. They all corroborated her whereabouts and arrival time at the party."

"But she was still missing when the deceased became deceased."

"No, the waiter she bumped into remembers her. So that was a complete waste of my time."

"Eliminating her from our enquiry..." Raymond mumbled, tossing the sudoku aside now that his concentration was smashed. He knew for sure he shouldn't have two 9s on the same line.

"But it revealed a useful detail. A couple of witnesses recall our favourite DJ having a heated conversation, slash, altercation, with somebody shortly before things went wrong."

"Who was it?"

"Nobody knows. It was a man who doesn't fit any description of the attendees we've processed."

Raymond felt as if he'd just been sideswiped. "He'd left before we arrived. Terry Hardman said he'd asked everybody to stay, and the security guard claimed nobody left early."

Sarah nodded. "We have a mystery man poking around

the fireworks controls. I've left word with Gary Mercer to get in touch to see if he can identify him."

Raymond nodded and reached for his mug. He spat the lukewarm tea back out. "Yuk! That's awful!" He stood up and pulled his coat from the back of his chair.

"Where are you going?"

"To get a decent cup of tea!"

*Time for Tea* was considered neutral ground, at least in DS Collins' book. Judith had agreed to meet him there on condition that he buy the cream tea. It was a simple asked, which he regretted when he saw how much the owner, Timothy, charged for such an ensemble.

"I didn't know scones and cream were considered a luxury item," he groused as he watched Judith lather a spoonful of cream onto half a scone. "I can't remember. Are you part Cornish or Devonian, Mrs. Spears?"

"Devon-ishters put cream then jam. I am neither. This half is a cream foundation. The next will be jam and never the twain shall meet."

"That's indecent," he said, cutting his own scone neatly in half and decorating it with the art of the Cornish.

"And it's Ms," Judith said reflexively.

"Ah, so I remember. But it was Mrs?"

Judith raised her scone half. "Cheers. And is there a reason you're bribing me with a cream tea?"

At the word 'bribe,' DS Collins almost choked on scone crumbs. He coughed and spluttered until he gulped down a mouthful of refreshingly warm tea.

"Hardly a bribe!"

"Slip of the vernacular." Judith smiled. "So, how is our investigation progressing?"

The detective resisted the urge to correct her possessiveness.

"That wouldn't be proper for me to discuss. After all, you are working for one of the potential..." he floundered, trying to avoid the word *suspects*.

"Terry can't be a suspect. He has an alibi. Me."

"That's not as watertight as you may imagine. And it should indicate what I can and cannot tell you." He shuddered with delight as he took another bite of the scone. It was the only thing he'd eaten since breakfast and the sugar rush was exquisite. "What have you discovered?"

Judith flashed him a shrewd glance as she nibbled her scone. "That's not a terribly good sign if you're asking me for progress." She had mused about revealing her discovery of the tablet bottles near the river, but thinking about it, she didn't know if they were medicine bottles or just the same shape. Terry Hardman was paying her because he was afraid of being set up, and such an obvious clue was triggering alarm bells. The fact that Stephen had taken her there further added fuel to her suspicions that he was up to no good. He was still the only one without an alibi, and she suspected the good DS knew that, too.

She took a lazy sip from her cup before answering. "We should both face up to the fact that Stephen Hardman is a person of interest."

DS Collins raised a quizzical eyebrow. "He was around the front, fetching something from his car."

That was news to Judith. "Was he now? And who vouched for him?" The detective's hesitation was all she needed. "Ah, I see. Still trying to confirm that, eh? Well I shall see what I can do."

"I didn't actually mean–"

Judith dismissively shooed him with her hand. "It's not a problem. And it will certainly help me find out who he was speaking to on the phone." She launched into her encounter with Stephen in the high street. Her voice dropped into a whisper. "Can you get hold of his phone records?"

"It's not that straightforward. This isn't *CSI: Little Pickton*. We'd need to arrest him before we could even begin that paperwork with the phone provider."

"Couldn't you just seize it?"

"Under what grounds? Curiosity isn't a legal precedent."

"Well, it should be. I might get it."

DS Collins' sharp intake of breath contained a sermon on how Judith Spears was not above the law, and he couldn't possibly condone nicking the phone and searching through it, and that such rank disregard for the legal processes was outrageous. Instead, it came out as a slightly high-pitched:

"Well, I suppose *you* could..."

"Mmm." Judith stirred her tea. "Although we are not sure if a crime actually took place." She gave him another shrewd look. Shrewder, if such a thing was possible.

DS Collins licked his lips. "Well, the bruising on Mr Hardman's, the deceased's, back hints he was pushed. But the whole family has mentioned that Richard fell many times because of his condition. Sometimes they caught him, other times they couldn't. That would explain the bruises, in which case, after the window was opened, nobody needed to be present to nudge him out. The coroner can't narrow the time of death. But it also doesn't rule out he *could* have been pushed, yet that doesn't fit the benchmark of 'reasonable doubt' we need. Likewise, he possessed elevated doses of medication in his system, but that could have been self-administered. So it still boils down to lack of motive."

"What if the siblings were to inherit a sizable chunk of money from their father?"

"Oh? And what have you found out?"

Without naming Maggie, Judith steered the detective towards Richard Hardman's business accounts. From his expression, this was clearly news for him.

"So both Rebecca and Stephen could be set to inherit life-changing money? It's probably hardly an afterthought for your client." He added.

Judith felt some satisfaction that she was helping protect Terry from the finger of suspicion. At least she was earning her outrageous fee. She was just waiting for a sizeable piece of information to present to him so she could justify inflating his proposed offer. She suspected where she might find that info, but her original plan of bringing it up with the detective now didn't seem so prudent as it had when he'd called her.

Their conversation had led her to where the proverbial smoking gun may be found. She just needed to execute her plan. And that would mean a sleepless night... and playing dirty.

# Chapter Eighteen

1 8

Terry Hardman's bellowing yawn came across as abhorrent over-acting designed to end boring conversations, as once had infamously happened when he met Princess Eugene, when in fact it was a purely natural reaction. The glance at his Rolex, however, was deliberate. And deliberately ignored by Judith as she poured him another whiskey. Terry raised a hand.

"That's enough for me. I've an early start."

"Nonsense!" Judith raised her own glass. "To your dearly departed."

Terry sighed and clinked his glass then put it back down without taking a sip. He glanced at his watch again.

"Shall I order a taxi?"

Judith tutted. "Your sofa is quite comfortable enough.

Sam Oman

Getting a taxi out here at the late hour is nigh-on impossible"
She patted the cushion next to her and noticed Terry's
eyebrows raised almost to his hairline. Before he could insist
on ejecting her into the night, she quickly added. "And when
you head off in the morning, you can drop me back home."

Terry couldn't think of anything to counteract Judith's
incessant upbeat attitude. She had unexpectedly turned up
at Terry's house in a taxi, citing car problems of her own.
She'd bustled her way through the door on the pretence of
updating him on her investigation. Not everything, of course.
In fact, she was more interested in questioning Terry than
providing him with any information. It had suddenly
occurred to her he was the only one of the siblings she hadn't
cross-examined in her own gordian style.

Terry was never usually the one lost for words. "I..."

"Exactly! What exciting adventures are you off on tomorrow?" Terry opened his mouth to respond, but she shot in the
question that he had so far avoided answering. "Oh! Is it for
the will reading?"

Terry thoughtfully flicked the rim of his tumbler before
replying. The clarity of the ring across the silent living room
declared it to be the finest crystal.

"You usually wait for the funeral before that happens.
The police still haven't released the old man." He sounded
tired. Or was it disappointed? He flicked the rim of his glass
again and listened to the fine tone, then threw Judith a look
that was loaded meaning. What had she heard?

Judith sipped her drink, reminding herself not to wince
at the taste. She hated whiskey and had artfully been
draining her glass elsewhere when Terry wasn't watching.
She needed him to be loose-lipped, not the other way
around.

114

"The detective mentioned to me they're still going through people's statements. You know how it is. Paperwork moves slower than a post office queue." She chuckled, then wondered when the last time Terry Hardman had set foot in a post office.

"They're suspecting foul play." It was a statement, not a question.

"They're the police. That's their first port of call otherwise they're out of a job." After the briefest of pauses, she added, "And isn't that why you hired me?"

Terry knocked back his glass. It was his third, and his speech was beginning to dance with the concept of drunkenness. "We'll my name isn't in the papers, so you're doing something right."

Judith smiled tightly. "No mean feat with Clive Wilson being here that night."

Terry Hardman shot her a stern look. "I didn't see him. I didn't invite him. Somebody mentioned he was."

Judith gave a light shrug. "Apparently, he was here and left before the police arrived."

"Are they sure it was him?"

Despite never seeing a picture of the man, Judith firmly nodded. "Without a doubt. If it wasn't you, then perhaps it was your brother?" She flicked a glance upstairs. "Maybe we should go and ask him?"

Terry made a noncommittal snort and drained his glass before planting it down hard on the coffee table. "He's spiteful enough to do just that. The sooner they're both out of here, the better now they've got no reason to stay." He stood. "I'm hitting the sack. I'm in London all day tomorrow. If you're insisting on sleeping there, there are blankets in the airing cupboard at the top of the stairs." He wagged a finger to the nearest staircase. "I'm leaving at six, so be ready." He motioned to the staircase and put a hand on the rail before stopping climbing up. He looked at Judith from under eyebrows that direly needed a trim. "Do you think somebody really pushed the old man out of the window?"

"You never told me why you think somebody maybe trying to set you up."

Terry thoughtfully drummed his fingers on the banister.

"Me and dad never really saw eye-to-eye. Growing up, we never had much, and he went from one badly paying job to the next. We lost mum when I was fifteen and he expected me to hang around and help raise the other two. That wasn't gonna happen. As soon as I was old enough, I headed to London. Got a job as a journalist and never looked back. He turned the other two against me. They blamed their crappy lives on me. He created a good old-fashioned dysfunctional family."

"Well, it looks as if you tried to make it up to everybody in the end. Offering them all a home."

"My dad's idea. I wanted to put him into a home." He caught her sour look. "I don't mean I was shoving him in some dump. I mean one of the best that money could buy. Somewhere he'd be able to make friends and have the best care on tap. Instead, he wanted Rebecca to be on the clock." He shook his head and lowered his voice. "That's when his condition deteriorated. I kept calling the doctor who kept altering his medication, but it never seemed right."

"Couldn't he afford his own care?" Judith asked innocently.

"Dad and money..." Terry shook his head.

"Didn't Stephen get involved helping him?"

"Ha! All they ever did was bicker. Especially when I

wasn't here. I'd get a call from Rebecca. She'd be in tears, as they wouldn't stop hurling abuse at each other. Not that she would ever admit that. She's not one to rock the boat."

"What were they arguing about?"

"Dad was annoyed with Stephen hanging around. Said it was like having a vulture keeping an eye on him. I didn't want him here either, but I could hardly fling him out when he no place to live."

"Why would Stephen do that if he wasn't expecting anything from your father?"

"That's where things become complicated. Y'see, when I made some cash, I bought dad's house for him. It was where we grew up and he didn't want to leave it for somewhere nice. But at least he had somewhere to live. To make things easier, it was put into my name."

"Ah. So the house reverts to you."

"Is mine. One paper. I don't want the bloody thing. But Stephen, the both of them, have their own ideas about that."

"But that's not part of any inheritance if it's in your name."

"They think it should be."

*Motivation of a sort*, Judith mused.

After a long, introspective pause, Terry continued. "Are you sure Wilson was here?" Judith nodded. Terry ran a hand across his mouth and shook his head. "Bloody odd…"

He walked upstairs, weary feet clomping and wood creaking with each step. Judith tracked his movement overhead until the footsteps were absorbed by the house.

*Interesting*, she thought, *Terry Hardman is such a terrible liar. Who'd have thought?*

Yet again, there was a scratch at the back of her thoughts. An idea that was fermenting, but not yet ready to present itself. The more she learned about the Hardman tribe, the more certain she was that foul play was rife. But it was a well-concealed bout of it. She could see hints and suggestions of intrigue and plot. The only problem was, like a Jeffery Archer novel, she couldn't see how to tie it all together.

She gave it forty minutes so Terry could settle down, then she quietly padded up the steps, ensuring she evenly distributed her weight so that the wood didn't creak. It was a technique she was quite adept at, having seen it in an episode of *The Man from UNCLE*. One of the many useful life skills she had learned from spending a childhood in front of the television. Years of absorbing seemingly pointless drivel, and carving it into a rather wonderful life...

She paused outside the airing cupboard and listened carefully. The low rumble from the boiler was the only sound permeating the house. It was forty-three minutes past the witching hour and the Hardmans were all to roost. She'd downed a Red Bull, which was probably waging war with her blood pressure tablets, but it would keep her awake for the rest of the night. She opened the airing cupboard door and found several blankets piled on a shelf. She slipped one under her arm, closed the door, then turned the hall light off. Closing her eyes, she paused again to listen for any movement. When she opened her eyes, they had become accustomed to the dark.

She held her phone in one hand, her thumb poised over the flashlight button, but kept it off as she advanced towards Stephen's room. Pausing to check her stealth mode was still working, she cast a glance towards the far end of the corridor where another set of stairs led up to Richard's room above. It struck her that the house's central staircase, and the one that led near the kitchen, just covered the ground and first floors.

It was only the one nearest the front door that stretched all three floors. The perfect escape route for a potential killer. Straight down to driveway.

She reached the door to Stephen's room. It was closed, and she couldn't detect any light spilling from within. She gently pressed her ear against the wood and listened. There came a gentle *put-put* snore from within. Judith felt giddy. This was far too easy - or perhaps it was the percolating energy drink.

Her fingers wrapped around the doorknob, and she gently twisted it open. Luck was with her. Somebody had ensured the ancient hinges were well-oiled, and the door opened without a peep. She opened it just enough to step inside.

Light from a partial moon tickled through the net curtains, caressing a nest of crumpled clothes, pizza boxes and an open suitcase on the floor that was half-cram packed. Stephen lay face-down on his bed, gently snoring. His phone was on his bedside table. Judith made a beeline for it – the floorboard creaking underfoot.

She froze as Stephen grunted in response. She silently cussed as he settled down, then carefully advanced as close as she dared, stretching the rest of the distance to delicately lift the phone from the bedside table. She was feeling please with herself – when she heard movement outside the door.

Somebody was approaching.

# Chapter Nineteen

# 1 9

Judith thought Daley Thompson had nothing on her. With pure Olympian instinct, she dropped to her knees – possibly doing some imminent damage to them – and crawled for cover to the end of Stephen's bed, just as the room door swung fully open.

"Oi! Are you awake?" hissed Rebecca from the darkness.

Judith's heart was in her throat as she curled up, gripping the pilfered phone tightly. Her movements had activated the screen, revealing it to be locked. There was a text message notification on the screen, but without unlocking it, the phone refused to reveal who it was from.

Rebecca hissed louder. "Stephen!"

"Mmm..." came the groggy reply. "What time is it?"

"Almost one."

"Sod off."

Judith heard the bed springs creak as Stephen repositioned himself. She clasped the screen close to her chest so the light wouldn't betray her.

"Terry's going to London tomorrow."

"I know." The words were uttered in the veil of sleep.

"Why didn't you tell me?"

"You've been locked in your room, moping. Go back to bed."

"The detective left a message for me. He wants to go in tomorrow for some follow-up questions." She sounded worried.

"So?"

"And Aunt Gwen left a message..."

This time Stephen exhaled a long sigh. His voice sounded suddenly more alert. "And?"

"And nothing. She said she was coming down. Said we needed to talk."

"And what did you say?"

"I haven't replied yet. But–"

The bed wobbled as Stephen moved again. "Do nothing. Let's talk about this at breakfast. What about the solicitor?"

"That's what I think it's about."

A pregnant pause filled the room.

"I'm too tired to think," Stephen eventually said. "Tomorrow. At least he won't be here."

Rebecca seemed to hover around for a moment before sighing and retreating from the room, pulling the door too behind her, but luckily not closing it completely. Judith listened as her footsteps retreated and Stephen settle back down to sleep.

For ten whole minutes, she dared not move. Cramp

seeped into her right calf, and it was all she could do not to howl out in pain as she rapidly massaged the stiff muscle. Her shoulders ached, reminding her she was getting too old to be creeping around.

As her lower back grumbled, she heard Stephen's breathing fall back into a slow rhythm. Risking a peek over the edge of the bed, she almost had a heart attack, as Stephen's face was inches from her own. Even in the dim moonlight she could see the drool at the corner of his mouth. She was about to stand and return the phone to the table when she was struck by a thought. She angled the phone's front-facing camera at his sleeping face and tapped the screen. The phone recognised Stephen and unlocked. Delighted, Judith stood and opened the text message as she circled the bed. There was no name, just a mobile number that she committed to memory, followed by a brief message:

ALL SET FOR TOMORROW. YOU BETTER PULL THROUGH.

She quickly searched through his messages, but if there were any more, they'd been deleted as had his list of previous calls and emails. Stephen had gone to great pains not to leave any digital breadcrumbs on his mobile. Judith knew that was the mark of a man guilty of *something*.

She delicately replaced the phone on his bedside table, retrieved her blanket, and crept out of the room. Taking care to check that Rebecca wasn't still around, she crept down the stairs to the living room. Only then did she expel a long breath of pent-up tension. Her shoulder and back were griping, and all she wanted to do was lay down. But the Red Bull was still coursing through her system, and she still had a second part of her mission to execute.

Moving as silently as possible, she headed past the

kitchen, to the back door, and retrieved the Wellington boots she'd arrived in. Gasping as she bent down to pull them on, she then took her raincoat from the rack behind the door and stepped out into the cold darkness.

Mud sucked like a vacuum cleaner at Judith's boots. Minutes into her journey and she was already regretting tromping across the estate in the dead of night, in the middle of another fearsome rainstorm. She knew it forecast rain, but since arriving at Beaconsfield Manor, it had turned into a monsoon, a tempest, a flood. Driving wind angled the fat raindrops almost horizontally as they struck her. She focused on the mud in front of her, regretting that she was relying on her phone's torch, rather than bringing along something more substantial.

She retraced the route Stephen had driven to the river, which involved crossing a pair of cattle grids in the wet darkness and trudging for forty minutes in the pitch-black countryside. Judith was not one to be spooked, but she was thankful the rain drumming on her hood was drowning out anything lurking in the darkness. Three times she slipped in the mud and barely kept her balance. She radiated confidence while in the company of others, but was far too conscious of her middling years that a spill in a dark field could have bone-breakable consequences. Yet, in the world of Judith Spears, curiosity conquered fear every time. Which is why she was always landing herself in trouble.

She had budgeted thirty minutes to get to the broadband box, and ten minutes to poke around. Just over an hour in which she hoped Terry Harman wouldn't head down to the kitchen and notice she wasn't asleep on the sofa.

However, the weather front and increasing wind hampered progress.

Judith stopped to catch her breath and turned away from the brutish wind that was causing the silhouetted trees at the edge of the field to lash with fury. She made a mental note of where she was in the field – which was difficult with the feeble flashlight. It would be so easy to get confused and wander in the wrong direction. She reminded herself that she just had to head downhill towards the river.

Fifty-two minutes later, he heard the surging water before drawing close enough to catch the turgid water at the edge of her torch light. The river was in spate, worse than before as it crept into the field. The encroaching water was threatening to sweep away the bonfire she had come to investigate. Already water was only a foot away from the firepit the medicine bottles had been dumped in. Hurrying, she walked around the junction box, which was dangerously close to being flooded.

The rocks gave a welcome relief from the muddy ground. She kneeled at the edge of the firepit, her knees cracking like twigs. The rain had soaked through the arms of her jacket, so she was shivering, and her light kept bobbing. There were two brown medicine bottles in the fire. Old style ones, made from brown glass rather than the cheap plastic nowadays. With her free hand, she pulled a kitchen sandwich bag from her pocket and slipped her numb fingers inside. Keeping the plastic between her fingers and the bottles, she retrieved them both and pulled the bag inside out, so the bottles now sat inside and clear of her own fingerprints. She stuffed the loot into her jacket pocket.

She poked around the black charcoal remains of the fire, noting that several pieces of paper hadn't burned through, but were damp, charred, and illegible. If she used her imagination, it could be the remains of a checklist. A gust of wind ferried it from her grasp and out into the river. She'd had her back to the water, so was alarmed to see it was an inch from her foot, raising at such a pace she would have to hurry for higher land or risk being swept away.

Judith stood back up with more than a little difficulty as the stones underfoot shifted. The light from her torch revealed that the indentations from her feet were already filled with water. She recalled a local map in her mind's eye. There was a fishing lake three miles upstream, the direction the storm was approaching from. She remembered locals had to ford the road a few days earlier because of flooding – this new deluge was capitalising on that.

She turned to leave – only then noticing something further down at the water's edge. There were several white plastic strips. She frowned and picked them up, seeing they were slightly charred. There were odd things to burn, yet somebody had seen fit to get rid of it rather than toss it in the bin.

*Something nobody wants others to see*, purred Judith's inner curiosity cat. It was a voice she both admired, hated, and couldn't ignore.

The water was now visibly creeping up the rocky ground, consuming inches within seconds. She darted forward, stumbling in her haste to reach the plastic disc before the water did. As she bent and lifted it up, she felt the waterlogged stones beneath her right foot shift and her ankle twisted.

With no time to even squeal out into the darkness, Judith Spears lost her balance and plunged into the fast-flowing water.

# Chapter Twenty

2°

The icy embrace of the river would have been a shock to the system if Judith wasn't already mostly numb. She was rather annoyed that the first thought which flashed through her mind, other than berating her own stupidity, was the grinning face of Dutch iceman, Win Hoff, nodding and chuckling in his charismatic way. Judith had watched his TV shows during sleepless nights. Now, under his mocking gaze her breath caught in her throat as the world churned around her.

Smooth rocks from the river struck her back as the current carried her. She didn't waste energy in thrashing against the flow. Instead, she steadily exhaled in a stream of slow bubbles, which confirmed she was submerged, although she couldn't feel anything against her numb face. She stopped moving, conserving precious air, but at least she was not panicking. Her back glanced painfully from another rounded boulder – telling her she was at the bottom of the river. Even with sodden clothing, she wasn't heavy enough to sink. She was naturally buoyant. During scuba diving lessons on holiday, the metal belt around her waist hadn't been enough to pull her down. She quickly deduced the river couldn't be that deep.

*Calm...* she told herself. Panicking was always the key to disaster.

Using all her strength, Judith flipped around so she was now face down and able to use both hands to push hard against the riverbed. Her body shot up, knees rotating downward and cracking against rocks. With a reserve of balance honed from years of Tai Chi, Judith tucked her legs and thrust her feet straight down.

She immediately shot up, her head breaking the surface where she was able to suck in a lungful of frigid air. All around her was inky darkness, but she could tell she was standing in water up to her breasts. She fought the pull of the current, stumbled, and was immediately dragged back beneath the surface. This time she was able to regain her footing and pushed herself in the direction she hoped the correct bank was. She was rewarded moments later when her knee struck another small boulder and she was able to stand, this time up to her waist. With windmilling arms, she staggered forward and out of the water. She dropped onto damp grass and caught her breath.

Adrenaline, combined with the ongoing effects of Red Bull, kept the shivers at bay, but she knew that was only a temporary salve. She had to get back to the house and dry off. Rain continued to bucket down and in the dimmest of light she could see the water's edge needling towards her. She felt disheartened that her phone and the floppy disc must now be on their way to the next village. She couldn't even judge how long she'd been in the water. Had she been carried beyond the borders of the Beaconsfield Estate?

Questions crashed together in her mind but were suddenly silenced by a slight glow twenty yards upstream. If there had been a sliver of moonlight, she doubted she would have noticed, but in the Stygian darkness it was a lighthouse. She heaved herself upright, feeling almost twice as heavy in waterlogged clothes. Before she could even take a step, Judith leaned against a rock and shimmied her Wellington free of her left foot – along with almost two pints of water. She replaced it and repeated the action for her other boot. Now she could walk towards the light. As she hoped, it was her phone. Fortunately, it had been tossed onto the bank and landed screen down. That was now cracked, but the rear-facing torch was still fighting fit. A minute later and the river would have been the proud owner of her iPhone. Her good fortune continued when she saw the floppy disc was lying just a foot away. She held it tightly, assuming stuffing it into a wet pocket would do more harm than good, then she set off back towards the house as the river continued to rise behind her.

If possible, the rain fell harder as she trudged uphill, across the slick fields. Each step was a challenge weighed down as she was with drenched clothing. The adrenaline high was wearing off, and she shivered. Still, she didn't stop. If she sat down, she doubted she'd be able to stand again.

It took almost ninety minutes to make it back to the house, and she was relieved that nobody was awake. The first task was to somehow dry her clothes off before morning. There was a spin drier in the utility room, but that would wake everybody, even in a house as large as this. Instead, she retrieved the blanket she'd draped over the couch and wrapped it around her as she underdressed in the kitchen. She smirked that if anybody wandered down and found her naked in the kitchen, she could at least claim she was having a senior moment.

With the coast still clear, she placed her wellies upside-down in the sink and stuffed her clothes in the aga – remembering to remove the plastic bag containing the pill bottles and her phone. She made a cup of tea, then kept vigil to ensure her clothes didn't spontaneously combust. The nylon in her raincoat melted little, but she was soon satisfied when they dried out, but the material was scorched, and it had lost a size or two. Still, it was delightful to have cheated death and then to put on a pair of volcanically warm woollen socks.

With only two hours to go before Terry was due to wake her up and take her home, Judith had dried out and lay under the blanket, after swapping it for a dry one from the airing cupboard. Lying on the couch, she mused her next steps, and just how much she needed tell DS Raymond Collins.

The next morning, or afternoon, by the time Terry Hardman had dropped her off back home, she'd sat in the bath where she had fallen asleep twice, only to go to bed and sleep right through until half-past twelve. Then she awoke with a nose dripping so much that it threatened to flood her cottage. If the inevitable chill wasn't bad enough, the internet was down. Judith assumed it was because of the flooding. It had the effect of pitching Little Pickton back to the grim days of a bleak Sunday in the 1970s. Isolated, and with no means of entertainment. Or in Judith's case, research.

She aligned her thoughts. There was no doubt that something fishy was behind Richard Hardman's death and it must be linked to the inheritance that nobody appeared to want to talk about.

Stephen was the one with most to gain and had been acting so suspiciously, he was naturally at the top of her suspect list. And that grated her nerves. She didn't have a high opinion regarding his intelligence, but if he was guilty, then he hadn't covered his tracks terribly well, and that didn't match his character.

Judith couldn't summon the motivation to dress in anything other than her fluffiest dressing gown and turned the heating up to sub-tropical. It was still raining outside, although it was now more of a gentle patter. The local radio news reported on flooding throughout the county, suspended train services, and all the usual perils of rural English village life.

Running events through her mind, she was certain DS Collins was under pressure to advance or close the investigation before it caught the nose of the media, and she suspected that would come when the funeral was announced. It was at that point Terry Harman would be assessing her usefulness. The problem was she couldn't shake the feeling that something was about to pop very soon.

On a post-it note, she jotted the phone number she'd lifted from Stephen's phone. She didn't have to; her memory was very reliable. Even if it tended to add its own filters every now and again, but numbers had been a large part of her past life, and they stood like megaliths in her memory.

Her mobile had a signal if she stood close to the window, so she was able to Google the number in the hope of it was registered online. No luck. That left her with just one option, born out of boredom – ring the dang thing.

Dialling 141 before the mobile number hid her own caller ID. It rang three times before a man answered, sounded distracted and hassled.

"Yes?"

Judith put on her best telephone voice, one she had inherited from her mother that Propelled her into the echelons of Downton abbey.

"Hello, I'm calling on behalf of Mr Hardman."

There was a confused grunt. "Who is this?"

"I'm calling on behalf of Mr Stephen Hardman–"

The voice dropped to hissing whisper. "I told him, I don't have time for this right now!"

Before Judith could insert another word, he hung up.

"How rude!" she exclaimed aloud. Before she could give it a moment's more thought, she hit redial. This time the phone went immediately to voicemail. She was about to hang-up when she realised the mystery man had recorded his own outgoing message.

"You've reached Clive Wilson. Leave your name and number and I'll get back to you."

The tone sounded and Judith involuntarily heavily breathed into the microphone before hanging up. Cogs ground in her mind.

Clive Wilson. The critic who had it in for Terry Hardman. Stephen had invited him to the party, and the pap had left around the same time as Hardman senior had fallen from the window. The same time Stephen claimed he was in the front drive. As she thought back, she recalled seeing Stephen in a heated discussion with somebody. Had that been Clive Wilson?

Skulduggery was well and truly afoot, and she knew it was time to nudge the police into doing their job.

# Chapter Twenty-One

2¹

Sarah Eastly was perfectly dressed for the occasion. That occasion being her day off. DS Collins had regarded her schedule absence with a frown so intense it created its own fjords, which was apt as the progress of their investigation was glacial. With only the two of them actively assessing the evidence and witness statements, she had thought they'd wasted too much time poking into the backgrounds of Gary Mercer and Judith Spears. The Guv had a hunch Judith was involved, a hunch that Sarah suspected was born more from frustration. He hated vagueness, and to him, Judith Spears was the poster child that. So, to make some dent in the stagnant investigation, Sarah had come into the office dressed in a white t-shirt, jogging pants, new white Adidas trainers, and with her hair tied back. She exuded an air of sporty fitness, when in fact she had planned to sit on the sofa all day watching Netflix and stuffing herself with a family pack of Monster Munch. She aimed to make her boss feel as guilty as possible. Typically, he wasn't in the office. By the time she arrived, he'd left to talk to the coroner, leaving Sarah to make sure enough of the other officers and staff around her knew she had come in on her day off. Her strategy was wearing thin after two hours of cataloguing case notes into the computer. She was so bored that she answered the phone on the DS's desk and was surprised to hear Judith Spear's voice.

Forty-five minutes later, she was sitting at Judith's kitchen table as the mercurial lady made coffees from her Nespresso and eyed her with twinkling eyes.

"You have made little progress, have you?"

Sarah sighed, "You sound like the Guv." Only when Judith placed the coffee down and slid a bowl of sugar cubes across the table did she realise it was a question, not a statement.

"Well, there are many trees to bark up." Judith's spoon clinked the cup as she stirred her drink and sat down, and Sarah found herself drawn to the deliberate act as if she was being hypnotised. "And I dare say you've been slogging through the boring past of the likes of me." She laughed, so Sarah laughed too.

"Naturally. And a boring life well led, it seems. Terry seems to trust you, though. How long have you known him?"

"Ooh, almost over a week now." Judith smiled at the puzzled look on Sarah's face. "We only met at the party. As I told you at the time."

Sarah nodded. "Trying to fix a broadband problem, I remember."

"Well, I suppose the flooding will do that for me now. We're all anxious to know when the funeral will be."

"I saw a message on my way here. The body will be released to the family later today."

"Oh, that is good news. The family can get things in motion and have a proper time to grieve."

Sarah nodded again and sipped her coffee. She suddenly had the feeling she was being interviewed by Judith. She veered the conversation back on course. "What was it you had to tell me?"

"Ah. It was about progress. What did you have on Richard's medication levels?"

"There was a..." Sarah checked herself. "Mrs Spears–"

"Ms."

"You can't expect me to tell you confidential information integral to the investigation."

Judith feigned surprise. "Oh? I beg your pardon, my dear. I was told by the good DS that I was helping *you* with your investigation." Before Sarah's eyes could narrow with any further, Judith continued. "After all, he did ask me to get a phone number from Stephen's phone. And we discussed the elevated levodopa in his system."

Sarah hid her surprise that Judith knew so much. She'd read Collins' brief report concerning Judith's suspicions. He was a stickler for the rules, but with a case going nowhere, she wasn't too surprised he was calling in favours. Hoping she could get a snippet of information to help push matters along, she decided to see how far she could trust Judith. "The levodopa levels seem too high."

"Especially as he was no longer on that medication." Judith's smile broadened with Sarah's confused expression. "Levodopa is one of the first treatments given with the onset of Parkinson's. Yet he was on both donepezil and memantine. Both, rather than one or the other. Add levodopa to that and," Judith gave a theatrical huff, "his head would be well and truly spinning in the clouds!"

"How do you know what drugs...?"

Judith tutted. "It's all in the case notes. Terry said the the doctor had kept prescribing different medication because nothing was working."

"That may explain the toxins." Sarah looked thoughtful, then caught Judith's curious expression. "It's found in magic mushrooms. Some practitioners of alternative medicine think it can help with his condition. And with an estate this big, there would be mushrooms around somewhere."

Judith nodded. "The question is, who had dispensed the drugs, and under whose request?"

"Well, Rebecca was his carer."

"Then she should know. But..." Judith tailed away, gazing thoughtfully in the middle distance as she sipped her coffee.

"But what?"

"Mmm? Oh, yes, you are right, of course, dear. I was just wondering aloud who else that evening had access to prescription drugs."

Sarah's coffee cup rattled on the table as she put it down and sat upright.

"Gary Mercer!"

"Mr Mercer? The DJ?"

Sarah nodded, her eyes tracking around the kitchen as fitted clues together. "He works part-time down at the hospital as an attendant. He has easy access to them."

Judith hesitated for several moments before nodding her

head. "Yes. My thoughts exactly. That is why I was hoping you could look at these." She took the plastic bag containing the glass pill bottles from the top of the bread bin and carefully handed it to Sarah.

"What is this?"

"A proper pill container that somebody tried to burn, maybe without realising it was glass and not plastic. It's the sturdy old type. I found it in a firepit at the edge of the estate, along with some papers."

Sarah held the bag up to the light. "They could have easily thrown it in the garbage."

"But refuse collection is biweekly. And if it is the weapon of a murderer, why would they want evidence hanging around that long? I was thinking you may be able to take some fingerprints off it. Like they do on TV!" She added the last with a flash of excitement, which Sarah wasn't convinced was genuine.

"Where was this firepit?"

"Down by the river." Judith held up her hand. "And now swept away by the flood, so don't get too excited."

Sarah finished her coffee and stood up. "I have to ask *Ms* Spears. How much of this have you told Terry?"

"Call me Judith. Almost nothing. I don't see why I should bother a grieving man with nought, but the speculation of some old busybody, do you?"

"That's what he's paying you for." Only now did Sarah remember that Judith hadn't answered her earlier question. It added further suspicion that Judith Spears was deliberately navigating the conversation to where she wanted. For a few moments, she felt the same suspicion that was niggling her boss, but it was quickly washed over by a flash of sudden hope that she could connect Mercer with the death. She pocketed the plastic bag. "Thank you for this. And if anything else occurs to you, call me."

"I would love to. Us women should stick together, eh?" She smiled once again. "I know what it's like, even now. I was a young woman once, believe it or not."

"Leading a very average life."

"Exactly. Don't get me wrong. I pined for something more, like you, but that's not how things were then. They're better now, but still... every helping hand..."

Sarah refused a second coffee and left Judith's home with a spring in her step. Whatever the Guv thought, she could see Judith was an asset to the case, and if it helped her get a little respect in the office, she was a tremendous help to her career too.

Judith watched as DC Eastly drove away. She had debated telling her about Clive Wilson's connection with Stephen, but as she didn't know what it was herself, she thought it best not to mention yet. Besides, Eastly had been a font of information whether or not she was aware of it. Richard's body was being released, which now meant the clock was ticking before the story made the mainstream news. And that meant Wilson would soon be under pressure to release his story before then. A story that would somehow implicate Terry. She now knew that the police didn't have a firm suspect in mind. Her reaction to Gary Mercer had been very telling; more so because it was news to Judith, too. She had all but written Mercer off her suspect list, but his re-entry posed a problem. Terry had hired him personally. Stephen had even made a point that the millionaire was taking the cheapest option. Why would that be?

There was only one reason. Obfuscation. Somebody was creating a deliberate smokescreen to hide the truth.

The only question was: who?

# Chapter Twenty-Two

2²

Judith spent the rest of the afternoon attempting to leave Little Pickton. The five roads out were flooded to various degrees, and impassable for Judith's weary Cleo, lest it floated away. The rain had ceased, and the floodwaters were visibly receding, but it would be days before they'd clear completely.

She considered calling Terry and asking if she could loan one of his 4x4s but decided against it. With no trains or buses running, she was essentially a prisoner to rural life. Her intention had been to travel to London to track down Clive Wilson. Instead, she stopped by *Time for Tea* to research him on her phone. It had the best phone reception in the village, and she hoped that a quiet cuppa would keep the lack of sleep at bay, but that was wishful thinking. The tearoom was crammed with villagers who had been summoned by the power of gossip. It was standing room only. Judith found Charlie Walker and Maggie conspiring at the centre of it all.

"Have you heard?" gasped Maggie through a mouthful of muffin crumbs. The muffin was gripped in one hand, an inch from her face. Her other balanced a coffee mug as there was little room to put it down.

"We're flooded in?" Judith hazarded.

"No. Well, yes. Richard Hardman's funeral is in three days' time!"

"Three days? That's quick... wait, how do you know?"

Maggie waved her hand dramatically. "It's all over the news! He's being buried at St Nick's." Her head bobbed in the direction of the local church.

"He fell out of a window in Hardman's fancy mansion!" Charles added in a whisper that lowered the volume in the café. "They said he was pushed!"

Judith was alarmed. She glanced at Maggie, but she had given nothing away. Maggie was a place gossip went to die. Although there was the usual village tittle-tattle that something had happened during the party, it had been assumed the volcanic firework display was the culprit, as it was heard across town and agitated every pet within hearing distance. The more gruesome details had not circulated. It wasn't wildly known that Terry's father had lived there, as he never left.

"Who said he was pushed?" Judith asked. "The BBC?"

Charles wobbled on his conspiracy theory bike. "No. But *everybody* is saying it."

Judith was shocked. That belonged in the Guinness Book for breaking the gossip-speed record. "Well, *everybody* should be careful. Terry Hardman is notoriously litigious."

The threat caused ripples of concern through the café, and the volume lowered as the customers tuned in to Judith's conversation. She looked around, now suddenly the centre of attention.

"The last thing we want is a pack of lawyers descending on the village," she said with a tone designed to trigger alarm. Her mind was racing in all directions. Whatever Clive Wilson had been planning in holding back information was now in motion. She didn't have to leave the village. By the morning the national press would have descended on Little Pickton and Terry Hardman will be thrust into the spotlight. Which, for once, wasn't where he wanted to be.

"You've been in and out of there," said Mrs Patterson suspiciously. She had been one of the lucky ones to find a table and had been lamenting how the flooding had destroyed her floral displays before they were ready for competition. In her book, that was a graver sin than the loss of life or isolating the village.

Judith shot Maggie a loaded glance, which warned her not to say a word. "Indeed, I have to remedy Maggie's broadband problems, and therefore all of yours, too."

A murmur of sympathy rippled across the room. They were all victims. It was enough for Judith to get the upper hand.

"The main junction box is on his land. So I have been fighting hard for access so we can all get back to online bingo." She glanced at a bearded fellow in the corner. "Or Betfred for you, Mr Cudgel." The man raised his coffee mug in agreement. "And I know as little as you all." She ignored the doubt on Mrs Patterson's face, which further soured as a murmur of appreciation did a lap of honour around the tearoom.

"Good on ya!" Timothy said. "And I suppose it'll be a boon to our little village having a press invasion."

Mrs Patterson rolled her eyes. "Typical. And with the slaughter of my begonias splashed across on the front page!"

Judith silently acknowledged Mrs Patterson's moral weight of vegetation over potential homicide. She'd have to keep her eye on that one.

Charlie tutted. "Typical. With the internet bloody down, I can't even put my spare room on Airbnb." He caught Judith's look. "Journos ain't waterproof. They need a roof over their head too. And there's not much else here about."

"That's a jolly good point..." mused Judith. A vague idea swimming through her mind. She took her mobile from her inside pocket and noticed she'd missed three calls from Terry Hardman, who'd finally left a voicemail. She resisted the urge to call him back. Best he stew a little more until she'd shaped a plan of action in mind. She had three days before the accusations would tumble down on the family. She suspected Eastly wouldn't receive the fingerprint analyses from the pill bottle before then, even if it was pushed through as a high priority. Until then, she would just have to go with her gut instinct. It had never let her down in the past.

Well, not too often, anyway.

Judith excused her way out of the tearoom and marched towards St Nicks. It was getting chilly, and the moisture in the air was forming a veil of fog. She listened to the voicemail message. Terry sounded uncharacteristically worried.

"They've released my dad, and I had to set a date for the funeral. The whole bloody family wants to descend on it. And one of them might be a killer. I really feel it. It couldn't have been an accident. Look... I'll be back late tonight. Let's speak tomorrow."

Judith had stopped at a pelican crossing to listen, despite there being no cars on the road. She replayed the message, concentrating on his tone more than the words. He was certainly stressed. Why would releasing his father's body for burial be more stressful than the police holding it back pending a murder inquiry? He surely couldn't be concerned by the press attention. That was the sort of thing he thrived on. Hardman had the skill of squeezing sympathy for himself out of the most uncomfortable news, so that couldn't be a cause for extra concern.

Or was he worried that the police suspected him?

Judith put the phone away and crossed the road as she continued towards the church. She recalled the order of events from that night. She'd heard Terry and Rebecca talking in the living room. Roughly the same time, Clive Wilson would shortly leave via the front door. Which indicated he was in the house too with Stephen.

Did Clive Wilson and Richard Harman know one another?

DJ Gary Mercer had wondered away from his deck because Terry Hardman hadn't told him to start. Then it had gone wrong, and Richard Hardman tumbled from the window. Possibly shoved, or tripped on a rug which was since moved.

Then, Stephen was aiming to quickly leave the country, a plan no doubt put on hold pending the funeral. A funeral which would trigger the will reading and reveal the state of the inheritance he needed. And he was in contact with Clive Wilson – a man who wanted to bring down Terry's career.

Everything was stacking up against Stephen. Except

Rebecca was in the same financial boat and was the one in charge of Richard's medication. As the church's rusty-red stone wall came into view, Judith started to wonder where DS Collins' investigation was leading him. She hoped by feeding DC Eastly some information, it would trigger a reaction. Although she hadn't intended to, she was becoming increasingly attached to the idea of proving Terry's innocence. She had never been a fan of his, but she was drawn to his constant railing against mainstream opinion. Not that Judith considered herself an anarchist, but she had never really respected authority and she appreciated that in Terry. She wasn't a fan of injustice either, so if somebody was really poised to set Terry Hardman up, that rankled.

She walked along the crookedly paved path that led to the church. No amount of fundraisers had ever managed to repave the treacherous path into church. Several roofs had come and gone, but the church entrance remained a gauntlet the unwary had to navigate for redemption. Judith suspected that the moss-covered headstones lining the path had a couple of victims who had taken a fatal spill on that very path.

A chill ran through her as she stepped over the threshold. Not that she was part vampire, but there was a definite drop in temperature. She was never one for religion. She had no opinions either way and was always fascinated by other cultures, but she lived by the holistic concept that people should be focused on being alive, rather than worrying about what came next.

Judith felt a shudder as she entered the chilly nave. A pair of stone angels glared down in what she had been assured was a benevolent gaze, but she found it hollow and accusing. But perhaps that was just a mirror into her own psyche.

Father Largy was tidying the altar. He had his back to Judith and was stooped over. His real name was Father Patrick Largest, ideally pronounced with a French flourish. But somewhere along the way, his parish had whittled that down to Largy - again pronounced with a Franco inflection because nobody here was a Little Britainer. The nickname didn't reflect the man. He was a lean, taut, and always led the pack in the various running events that ravished the county. If anything, he had ripened in a Clooney-esque way as he entered his early fifties.

Aware that she was walking with the stealth of a panther, Judith called out. "Father."

Father Largy folded upright to his full six-foot-two frame but didn't turn around.

"Ah! Could that be the tinkling ear-honey of Judith Spears?" He sharply turned around, a smile lighting up his face. "It is! You crossed the threshold and didn't combust into flames. I'm so delighted!"

Judith shot him a bemused smirk. The good father was a huge fan of the old British Hammer Horror films and often sneaked references into sermons for his own amusement. He equated Judith's reluctance to regularly attended services to the trials and tribulations of Christopher Lee's Dracula.

"Steady on, Van Helsing," Judith quipped. "I hope I'm not disturbing you."

"Actually, I was about to cast out for volunteers to help spruce the place up." The hint was deliberately heavy-handed.

"Good luck with that. For the celebrity funeral, I take it?"

"Oh, you've heard?"

"The village is abuzz with tattle. I think you'll be keeping back nosy volunteers with pitchforks if you're not careful. Although I would suggest Richard Hardman is hardly a celebrity."

"I have been warned that there will be a huge media bandwagon following it." His voice dropped to an echoing whisper. "Pushed from a window, I heard."

"Pushed? Not fell? Interesting choice of words."

Farther Largy circled the altar as he pointed towards the heavens. "The almighty sees all."

"Then perhaps the police should interview him?" Largy gave an awkward cough, prompting Judith to change subject. "I have been helping the police get to the bottom of the truth." She caught his quizzical look. "I was at the party when it happened. Along with all his family," she quickly added when his eyebrows shot up.

"So what happened?"

"That's confidential. Needless to say, it's important that I attend the service here."

"It's family only, I'm afraid."

Judith didn't doubt that Terry Hardman wouldn't object to her presence, but she reckoned it would raise concerns from the other two – and they're the ones she wanted to watch.

"I'm sure there is something you can do. After all, this is your jurisdiction." She gestured around.

"Not quite *mine*. I am but a caretaker."

Judith rolled her eyes. "Surely you can arrange something."

Father Largy's eyes bobbed around the church as a thought struck him. Judith didn't like the look of the smile spreading across his face.

"As I said, I am looking for some assistance…"

He held the duster in his forefinger and thumb and dangled it in front of Judith. With a wary sigh, she took it.

"Just what needs cleaning, exactly?"

Father Largy's smile broadened. "Everything."

# Chapter Twenty-Three

2³

The days leading to the funeral were packed with frustration and an aching back for Judith Spears. She sacrificed two days on the altar of priming up St Nick's church under Father Largy's instruction, that was more akin to a Tin Pot Dictator than she would have given him credit for, but it gained her assurances that she would be at the funeral, seating mourners. A role that the Hardman family could hardly protest about.

Terry Hardman returned to his estate, but didn't have time to talk to Judith, which was a relief, as she had little progress to update him on. The siblings were busy arranging the funeral and the wake that would take place in the house. Rebecca was spotted in the high street florist, ordering wreathes, and Terry had paid a visit to the church. Only Stephen Hardman was notably absent.

The flood waters ebbed, and the vanguard of journalists trickled through. The village had been unashamedly active in becoming as the county's biggest vortex of overpriced Airbnbs, but they booked up fast. Judith had even volunteered the spare room in her cottage, although in true fashion she had been a little more proactive than most. She would not leave her lodger to mere chance.

Exhausted from her forced labour in the church, she spent the evenings preparing the spare room, which was filled with boxes of mementos she had to cram in cupboards, wardrobes, and the loft. Spiders were forcibly evicted, and the lumpy mattress turned and reinforced with cardboard packaging between the creaking slats. If her lodger dared complain, then she could point out they had secured such luxury at half the cost the rest of the village was charging.

At 8:34pm, a good fifty minutes later, the doorbell camera alerted Judith her visitor was arriving, moments before the bell rang.

"Good evening!" she beamed, throwing the door wide open and gesturing inside.

"Ms Spears?" the trench coat-wearing man asked. His face was round, an affect amplified by his smooth bald head, that was bordered by a hedge of black hair above his ears that clung like thin moss to the back of his skull. A thick, perfectly trimmed moustache bobbed on his upper lip as he spoke. It drew Judith's attention, like a swaying charmed snake. He looked the epitome of what Judith was expecting.

"Clive Wilson? Please, come on in!"

The journalist carried a laptop bag in one hand and had a small backpack over his shoulder. Judith showed him to his room, forcing a smile when the corners of his eyes crinkled with disapproval. Then she left him to freshen up as she prepared a coffee and toasted some crumpets. She recalled him from the party. He had entered with Stephen. She was also sure she'd seen him arrive in the Mini behind her.

She had targeted the journalist with emails from a fake Airbnb email address she'd set up the very night she'd left the tearoom. It was easily done, and something she'd relied on in the past. At the same time, she'd taken photos of the cottage and quickly set up a page on the Airbnb website. She'd received dozens of queries because of the low price she'd set, but she turned them all down. She was fishing for Wilson – and he bit. Now she had him where she wanted him. A guest paying to be interrogated by the innkeeper.

"So, you're a journalist?" she asked, pouring him a cup of tea from the teapot she seldom used. She'd even put a tea cosy over it for added effect.

"That's right. As I suppose most people arriving are. What do you know about the Hardmans?"

So much for small talk, she thought.

"Oh, they keep themselves to themselves, really. Aside from the odd roaring sports car through the village. The occasional explosion and whatnot. It's nice to have somebody famous living here. What newspaper do you work for?"

Wilson fastidiously scraped butter across his crumpet. "Freelance. I sell my stories to the highest bidder."

"How fascinating! You must live an exciting life!" She sat down and regarded him in awe.

"It can be... yes. I suppose I do."

"And you must have a wonderful story if you're trying to sell it to newspapers who have sent all their journalists here, too."

She swore that his moustache shivered as he bit into the crumpet and eyed her slantwise.

"Lots of us are freelance now. Always looking for the angle, you know. Have you met Terry or his father?"

"Oh, the likes of me?" she waved her hand dismissively. "I met Ken Dodd once. Many years ago. Have you met him?"

Wilson shook his head. "Ken Dodd wasn't my type of comedy."

"I meant Terry Hardman. You must be such a fan to want to cover this low point in his life."

Again the moustache shimmied like a Hula dancer's skirt.

"He's an opinionated oaf. When somebody like him has access to such an ignorant audience, they need to be careful what they say. Terry Hardman is *not* a careful man."

"Ah, hoping to bring him down a peg or two, then. I dare say there are some here who'll be cheering you on."

"I think when I'm finished with him, everybody will be cheering me on."

"And is a funeral really the place to catch him with his trousers down?"

Clive used the scrap of paper towel Judith had provided as a napkin to mop the buttery grease from his lips and tash.

"They are the places family secrets tend to slip out. Were you acquainted with the deceased?"

Judith paused for effect and to adjust her upbeat attitude to a suitably sombre one. She would not let little things like *facts* get in the way.

"Yes. Not very well, of course. How could one really know such an enigmatic man? But I'm sure you know the family much better than me."

Clive's hesitation was so fleeting that a casual observer wouldn't have noticed.

"No. Just Terry and that is only in a professional capacity. What can you tell me about his father?"

Judith's eyes wandered the kitchen as she thought about how far she could mislead the journalist. Regardless of his stance on her client, and she conceded that his views seemed valid, she'd already decided that he was arrogant. While her mission was to keep Terry out of the spotlight, if Clive Wilson was planning to drag him into it, then she should make sure his story was so full of falsehoods that it would be rejected offhand.

"Dear Richard was a charmer, although that could all be down to his medication. So laid back and smiling. Oh, and a spendthrift too. Although where he got that from, he would never say. But he said it was his own pile."

Clive harrumphed and nodded. "Really? Word is that he finagled money from his famous son. More likely Terry was using his father to hide things from the taxman."

"Gosh? Really? That would explain a great deal, wouldn't it?"

Her mind was racing. She wouldn't put it past Terry Hardman to avoid paying his fair share of tax, and coercing his father into the scheme would be the easiest way.

Clive continued, warming to his character assassination. "And his divorce was a messy affair, too. She may have taken almost half of everything, but I suspect it was only the half you could see."

"He was hiding money?"

"Did Richard ever give you any indication he was under duress from his son?"

Judith suddenly regretted playing the lying game with a

153

snake. She had to tread with care.

"He was delighted to be spending time at the house with Terry. I suppose..." she hesitated and sipped her tea, giving Clive time to prompt her.

"Yes?"

"Nothing really. Just, I had a feeling there was perhaps something slightly troublesome with Stephen." She gave him a weak smile. "He's the other son."

Clive nodded and opened his mouth, but stopped himself from admitting he knew him. "Oh, really? Terry has never said much about his siblings."

"I suppose they don't mingle in your social circles." Clive nodded in agreement and sipped his drink. "So there's no way you would get to speak to them."

"Yes. A shame really."

Judith nodded in agreement. His denial cemented the fact Clive Wilson and Stephen Hardman were in cahoots. The nature of such cahoots was still in question, but at least she could make some solid deductions. Stephen had reached out to Clive Wilson, and the only reason to do so was to sabotage his brother's career. Aside from envy and spite, why go to all that effort? If their father had been keeping some of Terry's assets from the eye of the taxman and the ex-wife, then Stephen couldn't gain financially from such a revelation.

She'd have to ponder the implications some more. The funeral was tomorrow, and she was guessing the will reading would be days after. She should also check in with DS Collins to find out exactly what he was intending to do.

Clive Wilson was right. Funerals were places that secrets tended to slip. And she suspected that from tomorrow, a torrent may well start to flow.

# Chapter Twenty-Four

2<sup>4</sup>

The funeral was set for the afternoon, but the village was buzzing with activity from dawn as journalists set up camp around St Nicks. Clive Wilson made an early departure from the cottage after she made him a fried breakfast – only then discovering that an Airbnb was a misnomer; the last 'b' was never served. Then again, *airbed* didn't sound right.

He exited abruptly, leaving the bathroom in a mess. Judith was horrified to discover that the man left more curly hairs in the shower than he could possibly have on his head. She'd have to decontaminate it later. Her priority right now was to discreetly tail the journalist as he made his rounds around town.

With the high street bustling with activity, and a line of news vans parking up to broadcast the event, it wasn't difficult for Judith to remain unseen. She was disappointed to see that he didn't head towards Hardman's house, but instead milled around the tearoom, giving begrudging nods of recognition to some fellow newshounds. She was struck by the general reaction of surprise they regarded him with. He clearly wasn't expected to be seen here.

Twice he answered his phone and folded into a dark corner to have a heated discussion with whoever was on the other end. After the first hour, Judith was becoming tired following him. It was obvious he was biding his time, and it was unlikely Stephen would make a public appearance with him.

She was about to enter the tearoom when she saw DS Collins in a sensible black suit, and DC Eastly in a black dress that belonged in a cocktail bar. At least she had the humility to look embarrassed about that. Judith took a step towards them, but pivoted direction when she saw another familiar face scuttling through the press phalanx and into the church.

It was Aunt Gwen.

Judith made all the right huffing noises as she was stopped by officer Barry, the local uniformed plod who counted as local law enforcement on the occasional days he passed through town. He was joined by two burly community officers who were taking their job of keeping people out of the church a little too seriously.

"No one's allowed in," huffed one, who was apparently a woman.

Judith flashed a look of annoyance. "I'm supposed to be here, deary."

"That must be a first," quipped Officer Barry. "Nosing around for autographs?"

"Oh, Officer Barry, how I miss you bon mots!"

"My bon-what?"

"However, Farther Largy has asked me to assist at the service. Especially because I know the Hardman family and have been helping DS Collins on his you-know-what."

The community officers exchanged puzzled looks, but Officer Barry had made the deduction. The foul play surrounding Richard's death wasn't widely known outside the village, which meant Judith probably had an inside scoop. While he was quite happy to stall and irritate Judith Spears on any average day, he didn't relish a confrontation when she was correct about something. He gestured down the crooked path to the church.

"Then don't let me stop you. And watch your step."

Judith gave an affronted sniff of superiority and strode towards the church. She didn't feel superior, but she liked to rankle the constable every opportunity she got.

The church looked splendid, which was in no small part due to the hours of work Judith and a couple of other helpers had put in. Well-wishers had added a veritable forest glade to the proceedings. She found Gwen talking to Father Largy, who was making notes on a small spiral-bound pad. Judith waited until they had finished. Gwen turned around and looked at her in surprise.

"Well, well, look who it isn't," Gwen said wryly.

"Well, to be fair you didn't exactly ask me why I wanted to talk to you."

Gwen held up her hand. "Don't worry. The detective said you have a habit of interfering, and I heard through Rebecca that you've been hanging around the house at Terry's request."

"Trying to help you all," Judith said graciously.

Gwen's eyebrow twitched. "Is that a fact? Then have you already got to the bottom about who is wangling whose inheritance?"

"Ah, so you think there is a will? Which means you really think Richard had substantial savings."

"Which he said he was passing to me."

"But now...?"

Gwen's initial spurt of anger deflated. With a sigh, she slumped on a pew.

"Now I really do think poor Richard was being rail-roaded by somebody."

Judith sat beside her. "Who do you think that was?"

"Rebecca has been leaving messages. Little word bombs of accusations and paranoia. She thinks I'm going to take what's hers, and that Terry is going to throw her into the streets."

Judith recalled the measured voices she'd heard on the night of Richard's death. Rebecca and Terry had sounded worried, but civil, not like two rival siblings. And she was with Terry when their father died. So was there more than one bad actor involved?

"Why does she think this?"

Gwen rolled her eyes. "Because she has always had a victim mentality. She felt lumbered looking after her dad. It was supposed to be a way for them to spend more time together. At least, that's what Richard told me. She saw it as a punishment."

Judith painted this new view on Rebecca. A bitter woman, who saw caring for her father as a punishment, and the one responsible for administering his medication. A new angle struck her.

"How does she regard Stephen in all of this?"

"A waste of space. They were odd children. They didn't really dislike each another, but they operated around one another like ghosts." Gwen stared at the floor, lost in thought. Then she gave a little laugh. "I never thought about it before, but living under Terry's room must have brought back their childhood and she wouldn't have liked that. She'd probably see it as another punishment."

Judith watched Father Largy rearrange the flowers by mere inches in the worst attempt to eavesdrop.

"When is the will reading?"

"Still nothing from the solicitor. I know Terry tried to visit him in London the other day, but he didn't have any joy getting an appointment."

"So you've spoken to Terry?"

Gwen gave a horse-like dismissive snort. "If you count calling me up to swear at me, then yes."

"What happened?"

"Oh, just Terry throwing blame wherever he can. Apparently, he had a run-in with some journalist in London. I mean, when doesn't he? But he was demanding to know if I'd told anybody about Linda." She dropped her voice and stared at the back of Father Largy's head. "I mean, why would I? The family learnt long ago not to even comment about whichever girlfriend he was caught with in front of the cameras. That's ruined many a poor girl's life. So this one, I thought he'd got right. Not everybody knew. I wonder if Stephen or Rebecca knew how serious they are."

Judith wrapped her ignorance in a blanket of absolute complicity. "Of course. Discretion is a must. He wouldn't even point her out to me," she added.

Gwen chuckled. "She was the pretty redhead. Stayed at

the back of the room when the police arrived. They don't want their relationship on file."

"No, that wouldn't do," said Judith, although it was an effort to keep the surprise out of her voice. "But she was there the whole time. It's lucky nobody noticed."

"That's why she stayed in the living room for most of the night talking away."

Judith sat bolt upright. She had assumed Terry had been talking to his sister... but now it turned out it could have been this mysterious girlfriend. Which meant Rebecca didn't have the alibi she thought she had. She marshalled her thoughts back to the matter at hand.

"Why was he accusing you of talking about Linda?" she tried to make the name sound familiar as it rolled off her tongue.

"Because that's why the journalist was having a go at him."

"Did he happen to say who the journalist was?"

Gwen nodded. "His arch-nemesis. Clive Wilson. You'll find the two of them have quite a history. Especially because Terry got him fired from the paper."

# Chapter Twenty-Five

## 2 5

The floodwaters may have receded, but British Telecom were still unable to reach the village and restore the internet connection, which is what Judith needed more than anything right now. If that wasn't bad enough, the internet connection on her mobile phone was almost unusable because of the media circus coming to town. She needed to know more about Terry's new girlfriend and the acrimonious past between him and Clive Wilson.

Her first results drew up nothing about a new girlfriend called Linda, which indicated it was still a secret. After holding the phone above her head in the hope it would conquer anybody else's phone usage, she finally found an article about how Terry Hardman had sued a newspaper for events that led to his divorce. There had been a substantial financial pay-out – most for which went to his ex-wife, and the journalist who broke the story was fired. Clive Wilson. The incriminating article was hidden behind a paywall, but whatever it was had ruined Clive's career and appeared to make him toxic to even to the more notorious news outlets. Terry Hardman had ruined his life.

Funeral etiquette was not something Judith was familiar with. As a rule, she tried to spend more time on the *living* end of the scale than the *inevitable*. Which was ironic as she'd embarked on this late career as amateur sleuth which usually brought her in on ground zero.

She resisted her natural instinct to micromanage, and stood at the entrance as Father Largy instructed, handing out the service cards as mourners arrived. But first, as protocol dictated, the guest star entered.

The sombre tones of Chopin resounded from a corner speaker as Richard Hardman's dark-wood coffin entered on the shoulders of the four bearers. Grave-faced, Terry and Stephen led the way, hampered a little by their difference in height. A pair of blokes from the funeral home bore the other half, with Rebecca guiding the rest of the party in. She wore all black, with a midnight veil across her face, which Judith thought was wholly unnecessary in this day and age.

Terry ignored everybody as he shuffled one foot in front of the other as he followed Father Largy. She caught a flicker of annoyance from Stephen as he briefly glanced in her direction.

Thankfully, Officer Barry had the duty of keeping undesirables out, so Judith had the luxury to study the mourners who were mostly familiar faces from the party. To most, they would have been an inconsequential series of headshots, but Judith's sharp memory positioned them back in the garden, allowing her to build a mind map of where they were in relation to the DJ booth.

Gwen was behind Rebecca, but there was an obvious distance between them and no sense that either woman wanted to console each other. After a wave of family came friends and well-wishers who paid no attention to Judith. There was no sign of the mysterious Linda, and Clive Wilson hadn't managed to break through the police cordon.

People took their seats amid a gentle murmur as Father Largy stepped up to the dais and took out his notepad. Judith had peeked when he'd left it lying around. It was full of statements taken from the family that painted Richard Hardman as a loving, much-missed father. A cheat-sheet for the vicar who had never met the man but was now the one guiding out of this world and into the next.

Judith took a seat at the rear of the congregation so she could watch over the knave of suspects. Terry's head remained slumped as he stared at the ground. Rebecca's head occasionally bobbed as a hanky was raised to dab tears. It was telling that Stephen sat away from his siblings, on the left-hand side of the church. Although the details of what it told were currently an enigma to Judith. His head was like a meerkat, constantly swivelling to study the other mourners.

She was so engrossed in people watching that only the gentle creak from the end of her pew alerted Judith that DS Collins and DC Eastly had sat down. She gave a small nod of greeting and tried to ignore Collins' bemused expression. Her gaze returned to the back of the heads. She picked out Gwen sitting just behind Stephen, her gaze lingering on Rebecca.

Homages were delivered, prayers sang, and tears shed all in the name of letting a loved one go. Or at least a reasonably well-liked one. It struck Judith that she had heard none of the children say how much they missed or loved their father. As an only child, and with no children of her own, she had grown up to believe the environment in which children and parents declared their inner-most feelings was only something you saw on maudlin American TV shows. Yet she had to concede that people, even the British, did such things. Especially considering a death in the family. Yet the three of them had been silently self-absorbed. She felt a pang of pity for Richard. Did his family really care for him? Had they tolerated him just for his hidden money? On the flip side, had he been a good father? According to the eulogy, he had been extemporary, but the output of his loins questioned that.

A sudden wave of doubt crashed over Judith. Who would miss her when the time came? She'd had many friendships around the world when she was younger, but circumstance had led her to Little Pickton. Would anybody here miss her? Maybe she would get a plaque in the library if she was lucky. Or one on the BT junction box if it ever started up again. This was the reason Judith avoided churches and funerals. They were a reminder that one's place in the world was fleeting, and in her case, peppered with imposter syndrome.

She suddenly felt dizzy and tired. A feeling not helped by Father Largy's droning tone. She gripped the pew in front of her to help her stand, then made a quick exit. Only the two officers saw her go.

Outside, Judith gulped lungfuls of air as she leaned against the church wall. The damp chill revived her, and when she opened her eyes, she caught a handful of photographers taking pictures of her. She scowled and turned her back on them, but not before seeing Clive Wilson was standing behind the perimeter wall, further along than the main press bubble, talking on his phone in a hunched manner that loudly-screamed the need for discretion. She breathed deeply and turned to re-enter the church, but DS Raymond Collins was blocking her path. Judith gave a yelp of surprise.

"Detective! You startled me."

"The normally unflappable Ms Spears?" he said with a half-smile. "I didn't think that was possible. I saw you dash out."

"I felt a little off in there. I'm not a fan of stuffy churches. Or funerals."

"I agree about the funerals, but churches are usually quite nice. They help give one a perspective on life."

Judith noticed he hadn't stepped aside. She indicated the door. "I best get back before anybody else notices."

"I dare say they won't. Terry stepped up to give a speech. I bet it's seventy per cent about him."

Judith folded her arms. She could tell the detective was exploiting the opportunity to get her on her own, so she thought it best to commandeer the situation.

"As we're at the funeral, I take it there were no signs of foul play."

"Nothing conclusive. But you know what that means."

"Do I?"

"If you're the same Spears who lived in Scotland for a wee while and poked around in some frightful cases there, six years ago?"

"It does the grey cells good to keep busy."

"Yours must be firing on all cylinders. The DS there said you were helpful. He had quite a few nice things to say about you."

"It's awfully nice that you were seeking compliments about me."

"I wasn't."

"Well, I'm not bloody TripAdvisor, so I don't need to be rated. I suppose you were *eliminating me from your enquiries?*"

"Well–"

"So did I do it?" she snapped testily. "Or am I eliminated?"

DS Collins' mouth gaped fish-like. He hadn't been expecting verbal sparring. He spluttered:

"That's not quite the point, Mrs–"

"Ah, and my marital status rears its ugly head again." She placed a hand over his and gently squeezed. "I am flattered, detective, but I'm afraid you're just not my type."

Once again, Raymond Collins found himself confounded. He snatched his hand away and rallied. "*Ms* Spears, I am attempting to establish your character. I have perhaps over-shared on such a high-profile murder investigation and need to be aware of your credentials."

"So it is a murder investigation now!" Judith's face lit up with joy that she admitted was out of place during the victim's funeral. She quickly rearranged her expression to something more neutral.

Raymond Collins spluttered again, irritated by his own faux pas.

"Judith, please–"

Judith leaned in and lowered her voice. "I understand, Raymond." She pointed upward, momentarily distracting his gaze to the spire. "Those upstairs don't approve of private investigators getting tangled up in official business. It would look so unprofessional if they knew you'd told me so much. It may even prejudice the case." DS Collins went visibly pale as Judith nodded towards the reporters lurking on the side-lines. "And especially in front of that lot. It would be even worse if I cracked the case before you." She let the words hang, enjoying his discomfort as the bass-heavy singing in the church rose to a crescendo. Then she sighed as her devilish nature perched back on her shoulder. Despite her better judgement, she liked the faffy detective. "But don't worry. It won't come to that. I will make sure you get your man... or woman. Equal rights and all that. And you needn't be worried about me. I may have a past I don't want to re-live, but I can assure you of three things: I have no criminal record, I'm not an ex-spy like some old dears, and I certainly have no desire to take the credit. I'll work with you–"

Before DS Collins could fully open his mouth to correct *'with'* to *'for,'* she placed a finger across his lips and talked over him.

"And you can reap all the rewards. Believe me, I have skills you won't find in the conventional police force."

"Such has hacking a suspect's mobile phone."

"Entirely your idea. And *hacking* is such a loaded word. I merely looked at it. And can tell you that Stephen Hardman is up to some business with Clive Wilson." She looked slant-wise in Wilson's direction. He was still on the phone. "He's the furtive chappie with a head like a lollypop. He was in the house that evening, too. I saw him arrive." She took some delight in the concerned furrowing Collin's forehead. "See what a team we make? Now, let's get back inside before anybody suspects us of colluding in front of the press."

DS Collins took his cue and head back into the church. Judith paused before following. That had been a lucky side-step, but she knew it was just a matter of time before the good detective started to ask the right questions. Those would be more difficult to dodge. She felt satisfied that she had deflected him with the truth.

Well, two out of three truths were perfectly adequate.

# Chapter Twenty-Six

$2^6$

The funeral proceeded with the usual well-rehearsed monotony. Judith and the two police detectives kept to the back of the pack as the coffin was carried three hundred yards to a corner of the cemetery and lowered into the freshly dug grave, which was just within sight of the press cameras. Then, after a brief flutter through the journalistic gauntlet, it was off to Beaconsfield Manor for the wake, which was perfect timing as Judith's stomach was making firm demands.

"Cheese sandwiches by far," Judith said with authority as she bit into another precision triangle. She had latched on to Gwen at Richard Hardman's wake, and attempted to blend in, which wasn't a simple task for somebody who radiated busybodies like a lighthouse. She had briefly caught Terry and expressed her condolences. He had merely nodded in a deeply distracted manner. Rebecca too had traded a few words of thanks, but Stephen had artfully kept himself across the room. Every time Judith moved towards him, he would shift position like a conjurer. Twice she caught him throwing irritated glances in her direction. Now she was discussing mourning food with Aunt Gwen as crumbs of grated cheese fell to the carpet.

"Sliced cheese," Judith added with a sigh. "Who wants a sandwich that auto-destructs when you bite into it?"

"Ham," Gwen said, raiding the platter next to the cheese arrangement. "Can't go wrong with a bit of tinned ham."

Judith gave a shudder. "*Tinned ham?* What about real ham? Or vegetarians, for that matter?"

Gwen spoke as she took a half-bite. "Vegies have cheese. And who ever heard of a vegetarian funeral wake?"

"They must exist," Judith said as she scanned the room for any signs of Clive Wilson. "I know it's supposed to be a healthy lifestyle, but even vegetarians die."

"The dead ones won't be eating sandwiches at the wake."

"Good point." She spotted the two detectives keeping themselves to themselves in the corner of the room, and by doing so, they became increasingly obvious, like the proverbial elephant. Judith added: "And God help Vegans."

"I think we can all relate to that."

"It was a beautiful service," Judith said, reading from her internal bereavement script book.

"Really?" a man bumped into them both and mumbled an apology. Judith was too focused on their conversation to pay attention. Most of the mourners had already demolished the free wine, so it was just a matter of time. Gwen continued. "The vicar knew bugger all about poor of Richard. I added the bit about him collecting frogs. All bollocks, of course. Nobody batted an eyelid."

"I saw you looking around."

Gwen picked up another sandwich and sniffed with suspicion. "Tuna. Odd choice for a wake, don't you think? I should write a book about this." Then she looked slantwise at Judith. "Keeping a watchful eye on us all, eh?"

"Naturally." Judith's eyes strayed back to Stephen who was now ignoring an elderly uncle in favour of his phone. From his reaction, he wasn't enjoying what he was reading. He gave the uncle a curt snap of the head and started shuffling past people to leave the living room. Without looking, Judith snatched a tuna sandwich from the tray and pocketed a sausage roll for later and followed.

She assumption was Stephen was heading to the east wing and the front door, so she hesitated in the short corridor just outside the living room and strained to listen for the sound of the door against the burbling murmur from the mourners. It was the gentle creaking of wooden steps being quickly ascended that told her Stephen's business lay upstairs. She broke from cover and padded to the far staircase beyond the entry door, alarmed that the wooden floor squeaked with betrayal. Spreading her weight to the far edges of the stairs, she quickly followed. She knew this case led to the first floor, and not beyond to where Richard had been confined. She slowed her pace at the landing before continuing up. She could now hear voices, nothing more than hisses and heated whispers. Stephen and a man. While she couldn't make out the words, she was sure the new addition was Clive Wilson. At the top of the stairs, she brazenly peeked around the corner. The corridor was clear, and the conversation drifted from one of the side rooms. It wasn't Stephen's bedroom. Could it be Rebecca's?

The voices rose to hissing accusations. The shadows shifted and footsteps neared the door. Judith ducked her head back so as not to be seen and braced herself to dash back down the stairs – but the speakers continued down the corridor, away from her. She craned forward and saw the back of Stephen and Clive Wilson disappearing up the stair-case that led to Richard's room.

As quiet as a loud mouse, Judith stole down the corridor and into the vacated bedroom, the door of which they had thought-fully left open. It was Rebecca's bedroom, that much was clear from the strewn clothes, but it was not what she expected. There were few personal items on display. No photos of beloved pets, souvenirs from places that had left an indelible memory, or pieces of tatty art that invoked emotions. It brought to mind a monk's cell. The single bed looked far too small. A plain wooden wardrobe and dressing table had barely escaped the seventies. A pencil-case sized red make-up bag lay open on the dressing table. Lipstick, mascara, nail polish – all the usual suspects – spilled out. Judging from the condition of the containers, none of it was less than a couple of years old. The mirror was coated with a fine layer of dust that suggested Rebecca wasn't beholden to vanity, and that she probably couldn't identify herself in a police line-up. What were they doing in here?

Using the hem of her jacket so she didn't leave greasy fingerprints, Judith slid the nearest dressing-table drawer open. There was nothing but a pile of crumpled, but thank-fully fresh, underwear. She poked around, just in case, but there was nothing damning in there. She closed it and tried the drawer on the opposite side. That was empty. Odd. With the Jackson Pollock array of belongings around the room, Judith would have pegged Rebecca to be the type who kept her drawers stuffed to overflowing.

With a grunt, she knelt on a threadbare rug at the side of the bed and looked underneath. There was nothing but an army of dust bunnies were gathered in the corner. Judith recognised the possible signs of somebody suffering from dyspraxia, but before she could give that too much more thought she heard the hurried sounds of Stephen and Clive Own returning from their sojourn upstairs. Her knees clicked like the tumblers on a safe as she stood. The door was still open, and there would be no easy explanation for her snooping. She pressed herself into the small space between the door and wall and held her breath.

The door slammed shut as Stephen passed, startling her. Luckily, any involuntary yelp was drowned by the duo's footsteps hurrying down the corridor and descending the far staircase.

Judith expelled a pent-up breath and quickly left the bedroom, gently closing the door behind her. There was nothing obviously damning in Rebecca's room, so why had the men been in there? And what business did they have upstairs?

Judith knew she should re-join the wake, or possibly even follow Clive Wilson who was undeniably in cahoots with Stephen, and in the house without Terry Hardman's knowledge. The threat of blackmail hung in the air – but the revelation that Terry was dating somebody new was hardly worth murder. And *if* Terry had been speaking with his girlfriend when Judith was listening behind the door, that put Rebecca without an alibi. It was too coincidental that the men went to her room first, then to Richard's. Something was up. Literally.

Judith turned around and ascended the stairs leading to the second floor and Richard's attic bedroom.

A quick scan around the room assured her that nothing obvious had been removed since she was last here. So why had both men come up for a fleeting visit during the wake? What had they been hoping to find in Rebecca's room that encouraged them to visit here?

Judith slowly turned around, taking in everything. There was little point in searching for something unknown. Why would Clive Wilson need to see this room? Her stomach suddenly gurgled with a sound that usually preludes an Olympic dash to the toilet. A rush of searing needles surged through her stomach. Judith gasped in pain and clamped a hand across her belly, hoping the pressure would ease it. Within seconds her temperature rose, and she felt chilly sweat break across her brow. She had stopped turning around, yet the room continued to swim.

"Oh, dear..." she wheezed, before collapsing to the floor.

# Chapter Twenty-Seven

2<sup>7</sup>

"I've never had my stomach pumped before," Judith comment as she sipped a cup of black tea and wincing as it stung her sore throat.

Maggie shuffled on the plastic seat beside Judith's bed.

"They don't make these things for comfort, do they?"

"I don't think hospitals are really designed with the visitor in mind."

"I know. I saw the carpark charges! I hope they are going to buy an X-ray machine with what I'm payin'!"

"As much as I appreciate your visit, I don't want it to bankrupt you. Besides, I shall be out in the morning. They're just keeping me in for observation."

Maggie had diligently visited for the last two days and complained during each and every one, as was her way.

Although Judith appreciated the company, it was a sad reflection that she was her only visitor.

Judith had been found unconscious in Richard's room, in a delirious fever. She had been rushed to hospital to treat suspected food poisoning. Terry Hardman had texted her several times, asking if she was OK and wondering why she had been in his father's bedroom. She had replied with a simple 'yes.' Further enquiries revealed that nobody else had suffered at the hands of the wake's buffet. That hardly surprised her. She was gazing across the brim of her teacup when the scraping of Maggie's chair legs across the floor brought her back to the moment.

Maggie stood up. "I take this my cue to leave. Thank goodness you're not dragging me back here tomorrow!"

Judith followed Maggie's gaze to the end of the ward. Visible, just beyond the curtain partition, DS Collins and DC Eastly were talking to the Ward Sister, who pointed a chunky finger in her direction.

"Best of luck!" Maggie quipped as she lifted her coat from the back of the chair and hurried purposefully out, barely pausing in her stride to exchange greetings with the police. Eastly made it to Judith first, brandishing a paper bag.

"We come bearing grapes!"

"Grapes of wrath," Judith said, taking the offering and peeking in at the sensibly chosen green and red selection. Fat juicy ones, Waitrose, she guessed rather than the anaemic ones she'd bought at Sainsburys a few months earlier. "Thank you."

Sarah took the seat before Raymond Collins could catch up.

"Ah, Ms Spears. You look almost the same frustrating person we've missed." DS Collins' head turned as he looked for a spare chair. Not finding one, he pulled the curtain over to provide flimsy privacy.

"I almost feel my usual irritating self. Especially now that I'm official part of the case."

Deprived of a seat, DS Collins propped himself at the end of the bed, resting on both of his arms.

"You are indeed. Prowling around the deceased's room. Having a turn and being found there..."

"I was invited to the wake. You had searched Richard's room, so I could hardly be snooping."

DS Collins interjected: "I was quoting what the Hardmans said."

"All of them?" Judith retorted and took some satisfaction when he hesitated. That confirmed it was either Stephen or Rebecca. "And who found me?"

"Rebecca," said Sarah, who was leaning back in the chair with her fingers interlocked over her stomach. She appeared to be enjoying the back-and-forth exchange.

"And what was she doing there?" Judith caught the slight puzzled look between the detectives. It obviously was an overlooked question. "And who do you suspect poisoned me?"

DS Collins suddenly stood straight. "Poison you? Why do you say that?"

"The only person at the wake who suffered food poisoning?" She waved a finger towards the medical board hanging at the foot of the bed. Raymond's legs were pressing against it. He moved and read the notes.

"Who would do such a thing?" Collins murmured as he read. Then he met Judith's arch gaze and corrected himself. "Who *specifically* would do that in the wake?"

"Somebody who thinks I'm getting too close to the truth."

"It's a bit on-the-nose, isn't it? Poisoning you in the wake?"

Judith nodded. "Indeed. Perhaps it was orchestrated to make it look as if I'd taken some of the drugs myself? For some inexplicable reason." She took comfort that DS Collins shifted his weight from one leg to another, obviously uncomfortable and clearly at a loose end when it came to the investigation. Judith sighed deeply. So far, she had been enjoying the thrill of the investigation, but it had just become personal when somebody had slipped her a *Mickey Finn*. She needed to let DS Collins in on his own investigation. At least a little more. "I was there because I followed Stephen Hardman and Clive Wilson upstairs." That got their attention. "They spent a little time in Rebecca's room, then made a pit stop into Richard's room."

Sarah Eastly leaned forward, propping her arms on her knees. "What was Clive Wilson doing at the wake?"

Judith could hold her smile back. That confirmed the detectives had factored Wilson into their investigation and were at least aware of his bitterness towards Terry Hardman.

Judith nodded. "That is a jolly good question. My feeling is that he was chasing a story about Terry's new girlfriend." From the quick exchange of looks, that piece of information had evaded them. "Linda. She was in the living room when you gathered everybody for statements. A pretty redhead. And very possibly the one Terry was speaking with when I overheard him moments before Richard's death."

Sarah couldn't hold back a startled gasp. "Which negates Rebecca's alibi! The one you gave us."

Judith gave her a sad smile. "So it would seem I made a mistake. Although just why Terry and Linda's relationship should be so secretive is puzzling. It would all come out as these things do. What blackmail value is there for Stephen or Clive? I simply cannot see."

DC Collins hooked Judith's medical chart back on the end of the bed and clasped his hands behind his back in a more formal pose.

"Let me get this straight. You suspect Wilson or Richard of poisoning you... for some reason or other? But that would also suggest they are working with Rebecca, if she was the one who saw the old man out of the window."

"If anything, it muddies the motive," Sarah said, leaning back in her chair and staring at the ceiling tiles. "Two siblings contesting an inheritance, which nobody is quite sure exists. And Clive Wilson using it all to set Terry Hardman up... for revenge? It seems quite nebulous."

Judith gave a stark attention cough. "Don't forget my attempted assassination."

Raymond Collins spluttered an amused laugh before controlling himself. "Sorry. That just seems a bit *JFK*. Maybe at worse it was a warning signal. Or," he held up a finger, "it really was food poisoning? A bad tuna sandwich."

"Was Gwen standing with you at the buffet?" DS Collins said slowly.

Judith nodded. A thought had suddenly occurred to her, but it was so underdeveloped that she wasn't ready to share it.

"And of course, it could have just been one of those things," DS Collins said a little more firmly.

Judith couldn't hold back a sarcastic snigger as she waved the notion away. "Of course, dear detective. The psilocybin just happened to be in my sandwich and nobody else's!"

"The psilo-what?"

Judith nodded towards the end of the bed. "Traces of

179

psilocybin and Levodopa. It's written on there in plain doctor's handwriting."

Raymond took the medical board to read it again. "Which is probably why I couldn't understand a word of it." He tapped the word on the medical notes. "I just assumed this was the medication they're prescribed to you."

"Levodopa was another of Richard's medicines. When you're stuck in a hospital bed without a good novel to while away the hours, Google becomes your best friend. Psilocybin is a compound found in magic mushrooms."

Sarah shot forward in her chair. "That was found in Richard's bloodwork!"

Judith noted Sarah hadn't mentioned the empty medication bottle she had put into forensics. Which meant she hadn't told her boss and was still waiting for results. Judith nodded. "Indeed, experimental trials use it to treat Parkinson's. It's a hallucinogenic, and possibly safe in micro-doses, although the jury is still out on that. In larger quantities, it can be fatal." Judith pointed to her bedside locker and addressed Sarah. "Do me a favour, dear. Fetch my coat from in there." Sarah obliged and held up the black raincoat Judith had been wearing at the funeral. "Check the righthand pocket."

Sarah slipped her hand in and suddenly winced as she pulled out a soft, brown stick. "It's a sausage roll!"

Judith nodded. "Well done, dear. You're slowly restoring my faith in the police. I would like you to check it for psilocybin. I pocketed it the same time as the sandwich." Off DC Eastly's look, she added, "I was hungry, but Richard was hurrying out of the room. Run your tests on that. I think it would give you a sound idea of how accidental this all really is."

DC Sarah Eastly held the offending sausage roll between her thumb and forefinger and searched for somewhere to put it. With no help from her boss, she tucked it into the inside pocket of her jacket.

DS Collins drummed his fingers across the end of Judith's bed.

"So, what's your theory about all this?"

"I've presented the facts as I see them. I'm still grasping the string that pulls them all together. But I suspect Stephen has got wind that there is nothing to inherit, or at least he won't be getting a penny. So rather than leave empty-handed, he's working with Clive Wilson to blow the gaff on Terry and Linda. Maybe blackmail, I'm not sure."

"And he committed the murder?"

"It certainly fits, doesn't it? And maybe lay the blame with his siblings. Win-win." Judith looked thoughtful. "I'm missing something, though. And annoyingly I don't know what it could be. Do you have anything to offer?"

"Well. Um. No. To be honest with you, we're still circling suspects. I've pressed Terry Hardman for news on his father's will and he swears he has heard nothing. The solicitor in question hasn't responded to his calls or to ours. And of course, we can't force him to reveal the contents of Richard Hardman's will."

Judith gazed into the middle distance and nodded thoughtfully. Until a few moments ago, she was stuck in a dead-end, too. But now something DS Collins said triggered a memory. The detectives lapsed into small talk, which had thankfully lasted ten minutes when the end of visiting time was called. She thanked them for the grapes and ate a few as she waited for the ward to clear visitors. Each bite was a welcome relief, washing away the dry hospital food and the unpleasant taste of attempted poisoning from her mouth. But she was even starting to question that view of events. Things were not as they seemed.

A few minutes surfing the internet's more scientific forums for information on the use of psilocybin to combat Parkinson's and she had the details she needed. Judith fetched her slippers and dressing gown Maggie had provided on her first visit and set out to explore the hospital. Her first port of call was courtesy of Facebook.

Wandering the sterile hospital corridors in a dressing gown and slippers, Judith felt invisible. Which was perfect for what she had in mind. Slipping past the ward sister with nothing more than a smile and a vague hint that she needed the toilet was child's play. A map in the corridor was committed to memory in moments, helped by a little prior research online. Her destination was next to the dermatology department, so she followed the coloured guidelines on the floor. She took the elevator to the first floor, sharing it with a pair of attendants in green scrubs were taking a brief social media respite on their mobile phones, and paid no attention to her. She crossed from one side of the car to the other, bumping into one of them as the elevator came to a juddering stop.

"So sorry, dear."

"S'okay," mumbled the man who couldn't be more than twenty-five and whose eyes didn't lift from the Instagram video of a dancer.

Judith smiled as she stepped out and the attendants continued onwards, no doubt zigzagging between floors for an unofficial, and no doubt well deserved, break. She rolled the ID card she had snatched from the attendant's hip, proud that she still had the dexterity even in her fifties. She felt the old familiar thrill of mischief surge through her, something that she had missed for far too long, and she predicted DS Raymond Collins had already caught the scent of.

She'd cross that bridge when she came to it.

In the meantime, she glanced at the ID card. She doubted she could get away claiming the likeness of the charming black man in the photo, but hopefully it wouldn't come to that. Ahead lay the open reception area for the dermatology department. It was bustling with outpatients and understaffed nurses trying to manage the flow of traffic and the impatient patients' expectations.

Judith took a seat and blended in. It offered her the perfect view of a secure door further down the corridor, which was part of the nearby university's research department which published their research paper about their clinical trials using psilocybin to temper the Parkinson's. She wished her plan had occurred to her yesterday, which had been a very boring day, and now she was worried she wouldn't have enough hospital time for her stake out. She mused about feigning sickness to extend it but felt guilty knowing that she'd be hogging a much-needed NHS bed. However, fortune was on her side and only thirty-six minutes into her vigil, her target arrived.

Dressed in green scrubs and white trainers, he pushed a trolly filled with boxes towards the secure door and swiped his badge before entering. Judith approached from behind, reaching the door as it clicked closed. She tapped her badge, and the lock snipped open. She glanced around, before shouldering the door open and followed DJ Gary Mercer inside.

# Chapter Twenty-Eight

2 [8]

"Did you get your mixing deck back yet?" Judith asked in a breezy, loud voice.

Gary Mercer jumped so sharply, Judith felt like applauding his theatrics. He clearly didn't recognise her, which was fair enough, as she probably looked like some old fruit who had escaped the psychiatric ward.

"You can't be in here!" he exclaimed, wildly gesturing to the door.

'Here' comprised a large room kitted out with a bed and some serious medical monitoring equipment mounted on wheels. One wall was a secure glass-fronted cabinet filled with medication held in familiar glass bottles. Gary's key was already in the lock.

"Don't worry, Gary, I'm usually in places I'm not

supposed to be and often turned up where I'm definitely not wanted. Like here, for example. I'm sure neither of us wishes to be here as you steal medication from the research program."

"I don't know what you–"

Judith waved her hand in front of his face to silence him, while the other hand lifted the flap of a box on the trolley. It was empty.

"I'm sure you think a university's research inventory is not as strictly controlled as the hospital's. And no doubt students are easier to blame. Or is it because this is the only place you can get your hands on the magical part of magic mushrooms?"

"I... I..." Gary's jaw worked independently of his brain as he frantically tried to recall why this old bint looked familiar.

"I suppose one can't blame you for seeking a bit more income these days, and nicking it is a lot less bother than crawling around a forest on your hands and knees finding the right fungi. I suppose these days you'd get kneecapped for trying to sell half-a-dozen portobellos on the street these days."

She saw recollection clicked into place across Gary Mercer's face. "You're with the fuzz!" The implication of this crashed around on him, and tears formed in the corners of his eyes. "I ain't done nothing, honest! I was just... just..."

Judith flashed the stolen ID card in his face, too close for him to make out any details and, in his flummoxed state, it just fed into the delusion he was talking to a policewoman. Judith felt on firmer ground, discombobulation was an art form she had mastered long ago.

"Now, now, now, Gary. Let's stop this before your mouth drives you into deeper trouble. We know all about the psilocybin you sold to the estate." Judith recalled all the tricks as if she'd used them yesterday, which wasn't far off. The key was to be vague enough while presenting her hunches to give the illusion she knew far more than she did. *Estate* was a nicely vague – either the Hardman estate or a council one. It was enough to lead him on.

"Only a couple of times. And it wasn't my idea. I swear. It was for the old man. To help him. I was trying to help," he insisted.

"And getting paid handsomely for it?" Judith indicated the trolley. "And now you see a gap in the market. Even if the old man died."

Gary Mercer physically recoiled as the sense of wrong-doing sank in. "I had nothing to do with that! I heard it was an accident. I felt bad if he was tripping his tits off, but all I was doing that night was providing the entertainment. I swear."

"Well, it looks as if you're being set up, doesn't it?"

From the bowels of panic, claws of suspicion regained control of Gary Mercer's mind. He squinted and looked at her up and down.

"If you're a copper, why are you dressed like that?"

"I'm undercover," Judith said resolutely.

As wafer thin as it sounded, it seemed to do the trick for Gary. He put his hands across his face and sobbed into his palms.

"Oh, God…"

"In fact, aside from Richard Hardman, a lovely lady was also poisoned by a deliberate overdose."

Gary sucked in a sharp breath. "She just asked for it. Said she'd been using it for herself. For anxiety."

Judith's brain somersaulted. *She.* That would have been

confirmation enough to drop Rebecca Hardman straight into the firing line... if it wasn't for one simple thing that had been bugging her. Aunt Gwen. She had been grazing from the same plates at the same time. She had been the one close enough to pepper Judith's food with the drugs. It was an emotive thought, but part of Judith railed at the idea and insisted she look at both sides of the situation. Aunt Gwen could just as easily have been the target. With a sob, Gary Mercer was opening up like a torn plastic bag.

"You know, people like that are the sort to have all their excuses covered. It's easy for them to set you up, Gary. After all, somebody must take the blame."

Gary looked horrified. "I've never dealt drugs in me life! I stole a Snickers bar once from a corner shop and, and... and I bunked on the bus a couple of times. But I'm not a criminal. I just wanted to mix some music and have a good time!"

"You're the perfect patsy," said Judith sadly. She noted the confused look on Gary's face. "It means scapegoat." She paused to make sure he understood that term. "Look, we know you were not being malicious. After all, you didn't deliver the killing doses, and judges always take into account how cooperative a defendant is..." she let the words sink in, ensuring his fate was looking grim enough. "So, if you're lucky, you probably get a slap on the wrists. Fired, of course, but still..."

Gary's eyes widened with hope. Judith was speaking complete bollocks. Theft, tangential links to a murder, her own – possibly – attempted poisoning. Gary Mercer was set to do time behind bars, and she was adamant to make sure the sentence was for as long as possible. She had little truck with the grimier criminal elements. They certainly should reap what they sowed. But for now it was sensible to keep him on-side.

"Look, Gary. We could arrest you rest now, but that would alert them that we're on to them." Keep the vague disinformation flowing, Judith reminded herself. "I can see how much they're manipulating you to take the blame. Now, I don't think you're much of a flight risk, so my suggestion, if you're willing to cooperate, is to leave all this here." She indicated the trolley. "And take the rest of the week off while we get the real villains. Then, you can testify and recover your good name and get back to DJing. How does that sound?"

Garry nodded and burbled between sobs. Tears were flowing down his flushed cheeks. "Brilliant."

Judith laid a reassuring hand on his and smiled. "I knew you were a smart one. I'll tell you what, let's go to the canteen, find a quiet corner and you can recover your wits and tell me your side of the story. How does that sound?"

Five minutes later they sat in the corner of the hospital's coffee shop, sitting in an uncomfortable bucket seat. Gary Mercer clutched a latte, while Judith gently stirred an English breakfast tea served in an oversized cup. Gary had offered to pay when Judith pointed out her undercover disguise was so accurate that it came without of purse.

Gary gazed mournfully into the frothy heart of his latte as if the bubbles were the memories he was reluctantly dredging up.

"When I got the email, I thought it was wind-up. DJing for Hardman, that's like a dream come true. I love him, but how would he have heard about of me? Turns out recommendations really do work, so I must be doing something right. It was straightforward enough. The date and how much. I had a hen night on that night, but I cancelled it for him. I thought a bunch of drunken women throwing up over me equipment wasn't worth it. I bet nobody ended up dead at that party," he added morosely.

"You can but hope," Judith said with a shrug.

"Once I said yes, I was asked if I could do the fireworks. I had the kit. Done a safety course. It's all pre-set on a laptop. You just load up the launchers and wire the thing up."

"On your own?"

"Strictly speaking you should have a couple of people looking over things, but I know what I'm doing, and it was a private gig, so..."

"So you bent the rules."

Gary shifted uncomfortably in the plastic seat. Judith shot him a reassuring smile.

"We all do it. Did you go down to the estate to organise any of this beforehand?"

Gary shook his head and continued stirring the coffee.

"That night was the first time I'd been there. I met Hardman. He was a bit narky, shouting at everybody. I got a selfie with him and set up my gear. I had Equinox by Jean-Michel Jarre lined up, and it should've been straightforward. Hardman was going to do a speech, and that was my cue."

"But you were distracted?"

"It was supposed to start at seven, but by ten-past he still hadn't come over to me, so I went looking for him."

"And left your equipment unattended?"

"It wasn't like it was the sort of student party where they'd start messing around with the deck. Looked safe enough."

"Where did you go looking for Mr Hardman?"

"I walked through the party, then went around to the front just in case he was there greeting people. He had a few nice cars parked there. Couple of Porsches and a Bentley GT. So I had a mooch at them. It was quiet. There was just a car leaving and nobody else around. It was then I heard the music and fireworks crank up. By the time I legged it around the house, everything had gone wrong, then I heard the screams."

Judith sipped her tea and played his story through her head, positioning herself where he stood and trying to seek out what he could and could not see.

"You said there was a car leaving? Did you see the driver?"

Gary considered the question as he clutched the coffee cup like a life preserver and nosily drank with an unsolicited growl of relief as the coffee went down.

"It was a bald bloke driving a Mini. But I didn't see his face."

Judith tried to rein in the sudden thrill of excitement. Finally, an eyewitness proving Clive Wilson was leaving just as the fireworks went off. Then another thought occurred to her.

"Who recommended you to Mr Hardman? He is hardly the sort to have his finger on the pulse of local businesses."

"Oh, it wasn't him who emailed me. It was his sister. Becs. She recommended me."

Judith remained poker faced. "Of course."

"Yeah. That's why I thought it was a wind-up, because she said it was for her brother. But she paid the deposit, so that's when I believed it was a genuine gig."

Judith was dancing on the edge of an information black hole. She had to keep Gary Mercer convinced that none of this was news to her, and she had to dig deeper. Ambiguity was her weapon of choice.

"Of course she would persuade Terry. Although, how well did she really know you?"

Gary put the cup down on the saucer with a noisy clink.

"Well, that something I thought was just her being nice. Because she had been buying... y'know..." his eyes darted suggestively sideways. Puzzled, Judith simply replied with a gentle nod of encouragement. "Which she said was helping with her anxiety."

Judith couldn't help exclaiming as the penny dropped. "The psilocybin."

"I'd seen her a few times when she'd been in for tests, and we'd got talking over the months. I could see she was on edge, and she told me about her anxiety attacks. She was nice and her treatment was working. So I offered to help get her a little more. I'd been doing the donkey work for the university, so it was easy enough."

"You knew about the benefits of micro dosing."

"It wasn't like the NHS was going to prescribe her any of it. I was doing her a favour. She used a ton of it, and I didn't charge stupid prices. Like I said, I'm not a druggie."

A jigsaw was assembling in Judith's mind. Rebecca Hardman, anxious about her life and worried that her father and brothers were going to cheat her of any inheritance, started using psilocybin to calm herself. As things spiralled out of control, she used it to drug her father... or did Stephen discover she had the drugs and use that knowledge to frame his sister? There was no love lost between the two, and it would theoretically leave him with more to inherit. Had he planted the medicine bottle for Judith to find? Was he and Clive Wilson returning to the crime scene to ensure they'd left no loose ends in her bedroom, or to plant some further damning piece of evidence?

That still left Clive Wilson's motives in all of this – which were probably as simple as blackmail and revenge, unconnected to Richard Hardman's death. But then why try to poison her... or Aunt Gwen? Unless Gwen was hot on the trail of truth, too.

Another thought struck Judith. One she was annoyed she hadn't seen earlier, but blamed her fuzzy recovery over the last two days. Gwen had every opportunity to poison Judith. She was standing with her the whole time. What if Stephen quickly exiting the room was an act? He had been glancing at her, and it was an easy assumption to make that she'd follow him...

Judith's teacup rattled as she put it down. She felt as if she'd been played a fool. Was Gwen working with Stephen? The little rat's nest that was forming in the family needed to be untangled. They needed a shock. Something to force the guilty culprits into making a mistake.

She levelled a penetrating look at Gary Mercer as a plan formed. He tried to meet her eyes, but guilt forced him to look away. Judith had reached a conclusion.

Today, she would have to die.

# Chapter Twenty-Nine

# 29

DS Raymond Collins couldn't bring himself to speak about Judith Spears' passing. The words caught in his throat, which caused people to hurriedly whisper in surprise by just how close they had become. People found it endearing. The reality was Raymond Collins was a terrible liar, a trait that was required for the successful police detective, at least when it came to teasing the truth out of suspects. And there was a small part of him that *had* become fond of the woman, while at the same time he remained suspicious that there was more about her lurking under the surface. She was far too opaque to have an innocent past. With the absence of lies, he had developed other skills, such as being able to sniff out trouble.

And Judith Spears was trouble. Throughout the Richard Hardman investigation, he'd spent far too much time digging into her past and finding himself in a rabbit hole. For the average civilian, building up a case history was a simple process. Lives were governed by official certificates and bureaucracy. Birth, marriage, name-changes, death - everything was fastidiously logged and stored somewhere. The thing was, Judith Spears didn't appear to have *any* of these. At the very least, he was sure she had been born.

He was used to paperwork going astray and important documents slipping into the cracks of vast archives. But not *all* of them. As far as he could see, her life only extended back six years to Scotland. By her own admission, she had been married, but there was nothing official logged anywhere. Nor was there a death certificate for the unnamed husband. And, worse case, not even a missing person record if she had coshed him over the head and buried him under the patio. Raymond suspected that he hadn't existed at all. Other than a sergeant in Scotland vouching for her assistance in a couple of cases, Judith Spears was a phantom.

And that was irritating. Or as DC Eastly called it: *not relevant to the case.*

But for DS Raymond Collins it was an enticing trail to follow, like a line of chocolate buttons that he couldn't resist gobbling up wherever they led. And, because of her, he and Eastly were back in Beaconsfield Manor, reporting on Judith's demise. He reminded himself that it was an ill-conceived plan, and he shouldn't have listened to either woman. But he was the officer in charge, and he couldn't go back on things now.

Terry Hardman walked in from the kitchen carrying a wooden tray of drinks, and placed it on the low living room table, which was covered with new motoring magazines and a copy of Private Eye. Raymond wasn't used to the concept that a celebrity of Hardman's stature was capable of making something so mundane as a cup of tea, but he reasoned that even the most famous people got thirsty at inconvenient moments and were forced to fetch themselves a drink. He wondered if Hardman knew how to use the washing machine, and if he could share some tips.

"Thank you," DC Eastly said, as Terry Hardman sat down on the sofa opposite them. She pulled her cup closer and stared sympathetically at the pale brown liquid.

"Didn't know how you take it," Hardman mumbled distractedly.

"In a cup," Eastly said brightly. "So it's almost perfect."

"Where are the other two?" Collins injected in a more sombre tone to remind Eastly why they were here.

"Rebecca was out before I woke up. Stephen's some-where on the estate. He knows you're here, so he's on his way." Terry pinched the bridge of his nose between his forefinger and thumb. "To be honest, I can't wait for the pair of them to bugger off so things can get back to normal."

"Oh, they're leaving Little Pickton?" Collins asked innocently.

"Stephen has been moaning since the day he arrived. I don't think he ever unpacked his suitcase. And Rebecca..." he drifted off and stared into the middle distance for several moments before continuing. "She got rid of her flat up north. I think she might move in with Aunt Gwen so she can find her feet again. It's going to be hard for her. Not having dad to look after," he added.

"Can she go back to her old job?"

Terry shook his head. "She has been making plans with an old friend who moved to London. She wants a new start.

I'm surprised she's still hanging around, to be honest She doesn't want to be here."

"And you?"

"I've got a travel show to shoot in Australia in a couple of weeks. Around Oz in Ford Anglia. It'll be good to have something to distract me from all this."

"Has everything been tied up with your father's estate?"

Terry's head didn't move, but under his bushy brows his eyes locked with the detective's.

"Not exactly. The moment he was in the ground his solicitor contacted me to say that there was a clause in dad's will that still hadn't yet been satisfied that would authorise him to read it."

Eastly sipped her tea and did an admirable job of not gagging at the tepid stewed brew.

"That sounds rather irregular."

Terry nodded and pinched the bridge of his nose again. "Tell me about it. I don't even know what the clause is. He won't tell me, so how are we supposed to satisfy it? Now I have to get my lawyers onto him, and they're a bunch of merciless vultures."

DS Collins reached for his tea, then caught Eastly's slight shake of the head and thought better of it. "You must have some idea why there is so much secrecy?"

Hardman's eyebrows did a caterpillar dance. "Must I? You tell me. Sounds like somebody is trying to screw somebody."

"I was under the impression your father was a man of modest means."

Terry leaned forward for his own small espresso cup. "I told you I'd given him money over the years. He wasn't that hard-up, no matter what he claimed."

He sounded angry. Before he could continue, Stephen entered wearing filthy green dungarees, muddy Wellington boots, and a wax jacket stained with flecks of fresh mud. Terry took one look at the muddy trail he was leaving across the Wilton carpet and swore under his breath.

"Afternoon, detectives," Stephen said brightly. "The flooding has reached the lake," he said to his brother. "Everything's waterlogged."

"This isn't the time," growled Terry.

Stephen looked around. "Where's Rebecca?"

"London," Terry muttered frostily.

DS Collins cleared his throat as a sign he was entering official mode. "Thank you for coming along, Stephen. We are here to update you on…" he stumbled and shot a pleading look at Eastly. She put her cup down and took a deep breath.

"Judith Spears was admitted to hospital with food poisoning when you found her during the wake."

Stephen shrugged. "The nosy old trout shouldn't have been here. If she has any issues, then she needs to take it up with the caterers."

Any good-nature Eastly had kept pent-up suddenly evaporated with hostility towards Stephen's contemptuous tone.

"One. Your brother invited her here." A scowl rippled across Stephen's face so quickly that Eastly wondered if it had been a trick of the light. "And two. She's *dead*."

She let the words slam into place. Terry's hand wobbled, spilling his PG Tips as he uttered an unintelligible expletive. Stephen had the good grace to wobble and sat on the arm of the sofa to steady himself.

"Bloody hell," he exclaimed. "I take it back. She may

have been nosy, but she didn't deserve... How did it happen?"

Eastly's face soured as she examined each man in turn. She was enjoying the power-play.

"It was deliberate. Very targeted. Somebody had it in for her." She fixed Stephen with an unblinking stare. "And since you have just admitted how much you dislike her–"

Stephen jumped to his feet and splayed his hands defensively. "Hold on a tick. I didn't mean I wanted her to die!"

Eastly switched her accusations to Terry. "And as you invited her..."

Terry shook his head. "I think you know why I did that."

Eastly looked deflated when her boss suddenly took the lead. "You haven't been too clear about that, Mr. Hardman. I only have Ms. Spear's side of the story."

Terry sighed. "I wasn't convinced dad's death was an accident, and felt as if somebody might be stitching me up."

"You never told us that at the time," DS Collins said firmly.

"Because I didn't want to taint your opinion if I was being paranoid. You yourself said you found no sign of foul play. It was just a terrible set of ghastly coincidences."

"Why would you think somebody was to stitch you up?"

Terry gave a hollow laugh. "Because that's what people do when you have money. That's what people love to see when you're in the public's eye. No matter what you do, somebody will hate you for it. I know I can be controversial, but it's mostly an act. It's what people want. I get hung for denying climate change." He jabbed his chest with his thumb. "I believe in it. I've got bloody eyes. I might not completely toe the line when it comes to the cause, but that doesn't mean I can't see when it's snowing in August, or when my own estate is flooded! Over my career, I've built up so many enemies that I couldn't name a single one. They all blur together. That's why I needed somebody like Judith to poke around and see if it was all in my mind or not."

"Now what's your conclusion?" Eastly asked.

"I had thought it was just me being an arse. Now after this... well, let's just say the old paranoia is back."

DS Collins linked his fingers across his chest thoughtfully. He was enjoying himself more than he should be.

"That begs the question, what had she discovered, or at least what did her attacker *think* she discovered that was so bad they needed to bump her off?"

"Didn't she tell you?" Stephen asked curiously.

Eastly shook her head. "She didn't give a hint. I assumed you would know." She threw the question to Terry.

"No. She wanted to speak to me after the wake. Bring me up to date and, I suppose, get paid."

"You made a bit of a saving there, eh?" Eastly quipped.

Terry threw her a dark look. "That's a nasty accusation, detective. I think you've both outstayed your time here without my lawyer present."

"The vulture?" asked DC Collins. Terry nodded.

Sarah wanted to kick herself for being so direct. Raymond Collins wanted to kick her for the very same reason. While he had been against the whole charade, he couldn't deny that he'd enjoyed it, and it had given him intriguing insight into the brotherly dynamic.

"Just one more thing, Mr Hardman," DS Collins said as he and Eastly rose to their feet.

"You've turned into Columbo now?" Hardman snarked.

Raymond frowned. He didn't get the reference; he'd never been much of a fan of TV detectives.

"You have a relationship with Linda Furches."

After Judith had told them that the mysterious Linda was at the party, Eastly had traced the surname to the only Linda in attendance. A brief internet search had revealed she was a teenage pop singer. 'Star' would be a disservice to the term, who had a forgettable career. She had vanished for a while and resurfaced as a fledgling internet influencer. As far as Raymond could ascertain, that meant she got paid indecent money for talking bollocks for a minute or so. She had just over four million followers, which Eastly had assured him was an impressive amount.

Terry's poker face was perfect. "I know her."

Raymond pressed on. "How long have you two been romantically involved?"

"That is not a relevant question."

"It could be."

"I say it's not. Goodbye."

On their way across the front driveway, Raymond Collins couldn't hold back his smile. Eastly looked at him sidelong.

"You enjoyed that, didn't you?"

"More than you can imagine." He puffed his cheeks and exhaled. "Judith's such a bad influence on me. And what did you get out of it?"

They reached Collin's car. Eastly mused as she gazed at the dark grey rain clouds moving in. "That Terry is definitely hiding something. And I'm beginning to suspect that he was using Judith for far more than snooping around."

"For what?"

"As a distraction?"

Raymond unlocked the car and nodded. A distraction

sounded about right. The real question was who she was supposed to be distracting?

"And I think we have to talk to Gwen next," Eastly said as she climbed into the car.

It's exactly what Judith had told them, and Collins had responded doubtfully. Now he had the ignominy of following her lead. He glanced at his phone. Judith had said she'd keep them posted on what she discovered in London, but so far, she'd been silent. He wondered what trouble she had unearthed now.

# Chapter Thirty

# 3°

It wasn't the first time Judith Spears had died, but it was always tended to be inconvenient. However, there was an undeniable element of gleeful mischief involved, too. And at least it wasn't a permanent arrangement. However, it made it rather awkward to travel from Little Pickton to London. Had she spent any time planning it, then she would have made sure she'd had enough cash in hand. Visiting the ATM for a withdrawal was no longer an option. Admittedly, she thought that was overkill, so to say, but she had her own high standards and didn't want to leave any breadcrumbs that would reveal she was very-much alive. Luckily, the cash she had pried out of Maggie had given her just enough for a return train ticket, an anaemic and grossly expensive egg and cress sandwich, and a couple of cups of tea.

She liaised with the detectives to check herself out of the hospital earlier, and for them to keep an eye on Gary Mercer. She was sure Mercer was wallowing in enough guilt that he wouldn't reveal her little lie, but one could never be sure. DC Eastly had been enthusiastic about her planned demise, but DS Collins' dower adherence to the rules proved a little more problematic. In the end, he reluctantly agreed to play along on the condition that he wouldn't be the one spouting mistruths. That was Eastly's role.

Judith caught the first train to London, which necessitated changing lines. For once, everything was running on time. Being back in the Big Smoke brough on a flush of memories, most of which she tried to ignore. A quick flit around the Tube, and she was within walking distance of Clive Wilson's house before he woke up.

He lived in an average terrace house on a leafy street in Kensal Green. Cars were crammed nose-to-tail along the road, and after a brisk march up and down the uneven pavement, Judith found the only mini, a red three-door hatchback. The parking permit confirmed it was registered to Wilson's address and something stirred in her memory. She'd seen this car behind her when she had first infiltrated Beaconsfield. There was little cover as a murky London drizzle descended, so Judith pulled up her hood and waited several yards down from Wilson's house, holding a dog lead she had the presence of mind to borrow from Charlie Walker. It was a simple prop that would instantly defect any suspicion from a casual observer. The biggest risk was that she'd catch a cold. With events unfolding so quickly, she was certain Clive Wilson wouldn't be spending the whole day at home, and somebody had to confront him. With only circumstantial evidence, the police had no reason to interview him, so it was down to Judith to fracture a few rules on their behalf, and after the state he'd left her bathroom, she felt a little revenge was in order. Especially after the three-star review he'd left on the Airbnb app.

After thirty minutes, the damp chill was making her knees ache, forcing her to walk briskly back and forth. She was blessed ten minutes later when Clive Wilson hurried from his apartment. He wore a dark blue raincoat and had a leather satchel slung over his shoulder. Before he put up his umbrella, Judith noticed white earbuds plugging his lobes and possessed the air of somebody lost in music. He made an easy mark for Judith to follow back to Kensal Green tube station and onto the Bakerloo Line back into London. Never once did he look around, so she was able to keep comfortably close as he alighted at Baker Street Station and ambled around the corner to a row of Edwardian-era offices with apartments perched over them. He buzzed a door intercom, shook his umbrella as he folded it away, and pulled his earbuds out. He even smoothed the border of hair flat at the side of his head. This was a man on a quest to impress.

Fortunately, the street was busy despite the determined drizzle, so Judith had no problem in blending in as she stood at the corner of the street and watched. After several moments, the front door opened. Clive Wilson's smile broadened, and his head bobbed with pent-up enthusiasm. Judith grumbled as Wilson's bald nugget blocked her view of the figure inside. All she could see was the flash of a hand. Then Wilson stepped in, forcing the door-answerer further inside. Judith quickly marched up the road hoping to get a better look and was almost mowed down by a mother pushing a pram, who was arguing with somebody on the other end of her mobile phone. Judith quickened her pace, muttering about using a phone while driving. The front door started to close, dashing her hopes.

But at the last moment, it suddenly opened again, and the occupant popped their head out to glance up and down the street. It was a woman. Judith stopped in her tracks at the sudden unexpected turn of events. The woman's gaze slid towards her – and only the timely passing of a double-decker bus prevented Judith from being spotted.

Judith spun on her heels and headed back the way she had come before the bus had time to move on. She didn't need to spend any more time tailing Clive Wilson. All the key pieces were now there. All she had to do was order them into a coherent picture, which was tough given the Hardman family dynamic. It was laced with subtle jealousy and animosity, no different from most families, she supposed, although this one had the added bonus of a secret and size-able inheritance that had come out of nowhere. The basic level of human nature gave Judith the only leads to follow were passion and money. The frosty Hardman interpersonal relationships had quickly ruled out the former, leaving plenty of scope for the latter.

Judith was so lost in her thoughts as she retraced her steps to the Tube station that she almost took the wrong line. The tangled spaghetti snarl of the London Underground map made her think of the crisscrossing strands of the case. No matter what shape she arranged them, there was always something that didn't fit snugly or feel quite right. It wasn't until she was at Paddington Station, waiting to board the train home did it occur to her that there was one strand she hadn't accounted for. One person who had threaded their way through the subsequent morass of events. And that was one Judith Spears herself. The very reason she was here wasn't coincidental. It had been engineered by Terry Hardman when he'd offered to pay her to protect his innocence in all of this. As she took her seat in the half-empty quiet carriage, she added herself to the mix. The train pulled away from the station with a jerk; a reminder that she was now racing towards the denouement that usually required the gathering of suspects and the pointing of accusing fingers. In this instance, neither would be easy. In fact, it would take a little manipulation... and that was something that Judith was extremely adept at.

All she had to do was make a phone call.

# Chapter Thirty-One

3¹

"We are gathered here today–" Judith began before Maggie interrupted her.

"You're not officiating a bleedin' weddin', darlin'."

Judith slowly inhaled, gripping the steering wheel of her car a little tighter. It had been a chaotic twenty-four since she had departed London with the crumbs of a plan forming. She'd spent most of the journey on the phone to both detectives, or more accurately, she'd stuttered between telephone reception as she travelled through the countryside, wondering she'd have more success in a post-apocalyptic landscape. Between multiple calls, half-completed sentences, and echoing lines, DC Eastly filled her in on how the Hardmans took the news of her demise. In return, Judith outlined her plan, which, as she suspected, DS Collins rallied against.

But Judith was nothing if not persuasive, or annoying, depending on your point of view. With so much to organise, and still playing the role of a ghost, she had reached out to Maggie on the promise that her broadband problems will finally be over.

"I'm trying to rehearse how to launch into my monologue when the time is right."

"That's the lawyer's job to introduce proceedings, isn't it? I can't believe you got him to finally read the will."

"Ah, about that. Well... there was a criteria... criterion? Or is that a theatre? Anyway, something had to be met before the will reading could take place."

"I thought you said Mr Hardman didn't know what that was?"

"That's correct. Nobody knew what clause Richard had insisted upon inserting into the will."

"So what had changed for him to agree to the reading?"

Judith took her time to indicate at the next turn and stop the car at the give way despite the road being deserted. "I had a word with him."

At first, Maggie thought that was as much as she'd get out of her friend. She'd known Judith since she'd moved to Little Pickton, and they had become fast friends over the library incident. Judith was a good listener and insightful, but the more Maggie thought about it, the more she realised she knew little about Judith herself other than she was a terrible cook, a worse baker, and a wonderful liar.

"More accurately," Judith continued, "DC Eastly had a word with him. I just helped *facilitate* matters."

Maggie's brow creased. "But how if nobody knew what Dickie had written?"

Judith couldn't stop a mischievous smile from spreading.

Bursting to tell all, she couldn't resist an enthusiastic bounce in her seat.

"Everybody assumed that the solicitor, a Mister Jarrod Hemsworth, would read the will once poor old Richard was buried. Only then did this mysterious clause come to light. One that apparently nobody knew about. That was the cue for a sudden panicked rush amongst the family. Surely *somebody* knew. And if they knew, they would logically be the chief recipient of the will."

"Who is...?"

"Remember, nobody knew about the clause. Because there wasn't one."

Maggie shook her head in confusion. "You've lost me, darlin'."

"Gwen had only heard rumours about her brother's will. Rumours that suggested she was a recipient, but the others had heard or suspected something different. Then there was Stephen and Clive searching the rooms at the funeral. For what? Possibly a will that had been overlooked. Maybe. It suggested that Richard had changed his will at least once. The only reason to do that was because of a sudden change of mind."

"Or somebody had changed it for him."

"You're cottoning on. From everything I've been hearing about Richard, I wouldn't put it past him to have inserted a criteria, or whatever the singular is. A simple delay just to put the cat amongst the pigeons. A little pressure from the police investigation revealed that to be the case. He wanted the buggers to suffer before the reading. Perhaps thinking one of them would overplay their hand."

Maggie punched the air. "Bring on the intrigue."

Judith patted her coat pocket, crinkling the folded

printout inside. "Thanks to you, we can." Maggie's contacts at the tax office had come through only that morning. "Most of the family probably suspected Terry was holding back, but he had told me how puzzled he was, too. It appears nobody had the complete picture." The window wipers suddenly screeched into action as it drizzled. Judith pressed on. "We know Stephen and Clive Wilson were working together."

Maggie nodded. "I still don't get why, though."

"You will. All in good time. And then there was the poison."

"By who?"

"The *whom* who poisoned me."

Maggie's face lit up with intrigue. "Oh! And that is...?"

Judith pulled the Renault into a layby and switched the engine and headlights off. Maggie gave her a questioning look.

"And we solve it all here, do we?"

"No. We lie in wait here. I'm dead, remember? I and you have to make sure somebody arrives at the right moment." She glanced at her watch, then indicated ahead. Just before the bend lay the entrance gates for the Beaconsfield Estate. They had a clear view of who came and went. And with no party, there was no security save the intercom on the gate, and Judith was ready to work around that.

Maggie was pragmatic enough not to ask too many ques-tions. Instead, she pulled her coat a little tighter and angled the seat back for comfort. The chocolate limes she produced from her pocket reminded Judith that she hadn't eaten since the morning. With nothing but the increasing drum of rain on the roof and the crunch of sweets consumed at such a constant rate they could have been Class-A drugs, the two women settled down for their stakeout. Judith knew the family was already gathered, so it was only a matter of time before the solicitor arrived.

Forty minutes later a black BMW X5 pulled up and paused briefly at the gate intercom, before passing through. Seconds later, Judith's Cleo coughed to life and with the headlights off, crawled towards the gate as it was slowly closing. As far as the Hardmans were concerned, she had joined the choir invisible, so arriving by stealth was paramount.

Plus, she had one final snoop to make before she could launch her own fireworks.

# Chapter Thirty-Two

# 3²

DS Raymond Collins was a man who enjoyed a good frisson, although he would be the first to admit that frissons of any kind were sadly lacking from his daily life. Particularly the sexy sort. Living in a mainly rural area, several villages over from Little Pickton, meant that modern dating apps, such as Tinder had a narrow choice of participants, and being the local law enforcement further added to his desire not to let the community know too much about his personal life.

He blinked, reminding himself that a reading of a will was not the time to think about his lack of dating life. He had other things begging his attention, such as why he kept listening to Judith Spears' idiotic plans. The investigation had turned up no hard evidence that Richard Hardman's death was murder. There were admittedly a lot of suspicious leads, but Collins had been around the criminal block enough to know that coincidence and intent were yin-and-yang in real life. He had been lucky that the case hadn't spilled into the media spotlight. With such a high-profile suspect at the heart, it could have been a nightmare. Somehow, his team and the family had managed to keep it contained. Now his superiors upstairs had been applying pressure to swiftly close the case. And he was happy to comply.

Until twenty-four hours ago.

One call from Judith Spears had blown the entire case on its head. To make matters worse, DC Eastly and the mad old crone had coerced him to go along with a plan that wasn't entirely within the guidelines of good policing. However, when he tried, he couldn't exactly pinpoint *what* they were doing wrong, and he'd been gullible enough to comply, and now, sitting to the side in Terry Hardman's living room he was hardly able to complain. It felt as if he was the one being stitched up.

DC Sarah Eastly entered with a tray of drinks, with Terry Hardman close behind carrying the biscuits. The TV star looked jaded. Collins wondered if he was feeling guilt from Judith's apparent poisoning, or nerves from what the will would reveal.

He took a black coffee from the tray and slipped in two sugar cubes for extra zing. As he stirred his cup, he studied the solicitor, Jarrod Hemsworth. He wore a sharp black suit, the cut of which suggested it was tailored and expensive. His London offices didn't come cheap, which made him exactly the sort of solicitor an ill working-class man from Leeds could never afford to engage. So the stories of Richard Hardman's hidden wealth must be true.

Hemsworth sat at the eight-seat dining table and, with agonising slowness, arrange three papers in front of him. Since arriving, he hadn't said a single word to anybody, other than a brief courtesy to Terry when he'd entered the room. Unbeknownst to the others, he had spoken to the police detectives, so silently regarded their presence with nothing more than a sharp stare over the lip of his black-rimmed reading glasses – Ralph Lauren frames, Collins noted. He accepted the coffee with nothing more than a single sharp nod.

Stephen Hardman was slumped in an armchair across from the table, one leg cocked over the armrest. His usual cockiness was replaced with a furrowed brow, his eyes twitching around the room. Collins didn't know what to make of the abrupt personality shift, but knew he'd take great delight in collaring the slimy bugger him for Richard's death. Rebecca sat on the edge of the sofa, hands folded across her lap with an air of casual indifference. As both siblings had a vested interest in the will's outcome, DS Collins wondered if she had made peace with the situation or if, somehow, she knew the outcome already.

Only Terry Hardman was anxiously wringing his hands, in between taking hits of his new vape, as he sat on the edge of the sofa's middle seat, Rebecca on one side, and the enig-matic Linda Furches on the other. His girlfriend wore a figure-hugging red top and jeans, which Collins felt was inappropriate in the circumstances. However, there was no getting around the fact that age had made her more attrac-tive. He couldn't imagine what she saw in the blunt-looking Terry Hardman, other than his considerable wealth and fame.

The last person to take a mug from the tray was Aunt

Gwen. She wore wellies and still had her quilted green over-coat on, as Terry hadn't thought of putting the heat on. She clutched the cup with both hands for warmth and her lips pursed tightly, while looking sidelong at her niece and neph-ews. There was no idle chitchat or catching up on events. What had needed to be said happened at the wake, and this was now a family quite content to scurry back to their own lives until they had to reconvene for the next wedding or funeral. Collins felt a pang of sorrow for Richard Hardman who had died amongst a family so focused on their own needs, he was little more than a financial adjunct. They'd take his money, but his name would drift into the recesses of memory, lost in time. A sonorous voice suddenly rolled across the room.

"Thank you all for coming." Hemsworth had a baritone that was at odds with his slight frame. "I can confirm that the conditions Mr Richard Hardman stipulated for his will have been met, so I can proceed with the reading of his last will and testament. But first, I require a roll call of those required to attend." He read the four family names, who each responded with a nod of their heads. Hemsworth made a note on his pad, then slid across a facedown document that had been lying to his left. He flipped the paper over, adjusted his glasses, and read aloud.

"This is the last will and testament of Richard Andrew Hardman, dated October third."

DS Collins made a note that was two weeks before his death. From the various statements, the will had been around much longer than that. It had been amended.

"The contents of my home are to be distributed equally amongst my family as they see fit." This bequest achieved in nothing more than a few quick glances and downturned faces between the relatives. Evidently, there were no treasures to be had there. "The rest of my worldly assets are financial."

He paused and looked over the rim of his glasses at the assembled gathering. They were all sitting upright like meerkats. All except Terry Hardman who'd slumped back in his seat. DS Collins thought that was the attitude of somebody who didn't have to worry about money.

Hemsworth licked his lips before continuing. "And now I have your attention..." the solicitor tapped the paper he was reading from. "These are Richard's own words." His eyes pivoted back to the will. "Now I have your attention, as you are all freeloaders, and there wouldn't be a reason for you gathering here if there wasn't something in it for yourself." He took in the gallery of scowls facing him. Only Terry Hardman gave a single sardonic laugh.

"That's dad for you."

"So that's where you get your arsehole genes from?" Stephen muttered.

"Come on now," Gwen cautioned. "No matter what, let's have some respect for my brother."

Another murmur rippled around the room and Terry Hardman became obscured in a cloud of vape smoke.

Hemsworth inhaled noisily through his nose, causing his nest of nasal hairs to part like the grasslands of the Serengeti. "So, my dear sister, Gwenny, will no doubt be thinking of all the fond times we had as children."

DS Collins was looking directly at her at this point, so he couldn't miss Gwen's weak smile and nod of agreement.

Hemsworth continued with a dramatically deeper note as he settled into his role of Richard Hardman's voice of vengeance. "Bollocks of course. You were a constant pain."

Gwen's cheeks flushed beetroot red as all eyes turned on her.

"It... it wasn't...," she stammered.

The solicitor continued. "But it was only when we both lost what we loved did we come together, at least a little. Maybe too late, but it was something I remember. Which is a rare thing for me these days."

Gwen wiped away a tear.

"That leaves my children. And what can I say about them? With me to the last." Hemsworth paused to look at the siblings. None of them looked too pleased with the praise, no doubt awaiting the inevitable sting in the tail, which came moments later as the solicitor resumed. "At least you were when you realised I had money stashed away. Isn't that right, Rebecca? Snooping around, you found paperwork you were not supposed to. Drafts of my will, bank statements. You made the mistake of telling Stephen, and we all know *he* can't keep his mouth shut."

"Ah, so much passive-aggressive bile," Stephen said with a smirk. "It's almost like he's in the room."

Hemsworth continued reading. "That money was given to me by Terry."

Terry slapped his palms against his knees. He was suddenly chipper. "Well, that settles it. I'm getting it back." He stood up, ready to usher everybody out.

Hemsworth raised a finger. "Excuse me. There is more." He indicated Terry should sit back down.

"Do we really have to listen to this drivel?" Terry insisted. "We all know dad had a mean streak, and I don't think any of us wants to sit here listening to his abuse."

"I'm eager to know what he thought about you," Stephen said with a snigger.

Before Terry could snap back, Hemsworth tapped the table for attention.

"The will has to be read in full for it to be enacted. So, please sit."

Terry's eyes narrowed threateningly. "You know anything derogatory said could be considered libel."

"Not if it's the views of the deceased," Hemsworth snapped back. "Now please sit and allow me to continue."

Terry shook his head. "I don't think this charade is legal. My lawyer should be here."

"The vulture?" a voice came from the doorway to the kitchen.

All heads snapped in the direction. Judith Spears leaned nonchalantly against the door jamb in a way she hoped the great detective Jessica Fletcher would have pulled off. Gwen's gasp was almost theatrical, and Judith took pleasure to watch Terry Hardman flop onto the couch with such deadweight the wooden frame gave an alarming crack.

"How...?" was all he could muster.

"I had too much to do for death to get in my way," Judith said as she entered the room.

Terry tried again. "But..."

"I was following leads. Going undercover and, um... defying the odds." She reached the centre of the room and turned to face Gwen. "Isn't that right, Gwen?"

"I'm not sure I follow," Gwen said, her eyes darting towards the police. "But I'm relieved to see you were not poisoned after all."

Judith wagged her finger. "Well, one of us would have been."

Hemsworth was on his feet, whipping his glasses off. "This is not the time–"

She cut him off with a sharp: "It's the perfect time!"

Terry pointed between them. "You two know each other?"

"We've spoken on the phone. All in my due diligence to carry out your instructions," Judith said.

"I didn't ask you to–"

Judith waved Terry into silence. "Oh, hush! I knew what you wanted me to do. You wanted me to snoop around and get under their feet," she indicated Stephen and Rebecca, "so that you could sort out your father's will in peace. Except you didn't know it had been changed at the last minute."

The silence that landed after comment was telling.

Judith turned to DS Collins and gestured to the room at large. "So what you have here is the old-fashioned 'bump the parent off to claim the fortune' rouse."

"What fortune?" snapped Gwen. "I know he kept some of Terry's money as an investment, but it was hardly money worth killing for."

Judith looked thoughtful. "That depends on your definition of 'fortune' I suppose. For a multimillionaire like Terry, perhaps it's a drop in the ocean. For the rest of us... well, eight-point-two million pounds really is a fortune."

Murmurs of astonishment broke across the room. Evidently, the extent Richard's horde was unknown.

Terry stood up and stabbed a finger at Judith. "Why are we listening to this mad old trout? She's making things up. She shouldn't be here! She should be dead!" Everybody's eyes went wide. He hastily backtracked. "Not that I would want that..."

"I thought she was on your side?" DC Eastly said between slurps of coffee. She had been enjoying Judith's floor show immensely.

Terry didn't seem to have a comeback at hand. DS Collins stepped closer to the solicitor.

"Is there any merit to these numbers?"

Hemsworth was loath to break protocol, but relented under the detective's stern gaze. He nodded, triggering further startled reaction around the room.

"Where the hell did dad get all that from?" said Stephen as he stared hard at his brother.

"Guess," said Rebecca, speaking for the first time. She could barely keep the hatred out of her voice as she glared at Terry. "You gave it as a gift, so doesn't mean it's yours!"

From her pocket, Judith fished the printout that Maggie had given her.

"Well, 'gift' is a rather generous term. These are documents from a tax investigation against the dearly departed." She held them up so Rebecca could see. "Do these look familiar? Isn't this what you found in your father's house in Leeds?" Rebecca tightly folded her arms and didn't respond. "Except they thought the amount squirrelled away was far lower."

"Judith," Terry said in a gentle voice. "This isn't the right time for this."

"When *is* the right time to discuss murder?"

"So it was murder?" DS Collins said, seconds before regretting it.

Hemsworth's eyebrows shot up. "You are a real detective, are you not?"

"Shush!" Judith snapped. "I require a little concentration to untangle the morass of deceit we're swamped with." She turned to Linda Furches and smiled warmly. "Miss Furches, a pleasure to finally look you in the eye and say hello."

"Hello..." Linda replied meekly. She tried to stand, but Judith motioned for her to stay seated.

"It's best you sit back and discover more about the family you're associating with." Judith's smile faded as she took in the room. "Poor Richard was murdered. He was killed because someone thought he'd outlived his usefulness. Because his Parkinson's was becoming too much to cope with. And because he was worth much more dead than alive. That is, if he could be parted from his money before the taxman. With his death documents would become lost, debts don't pass on to family any longer or most of us would be in debtor's jail."

"Tell me about it," DC Eastly said, rolling her eyes before flushing with embarrassment for speaking her thoughts out loud. "My mum lives on her credit cards," she said by way of explanation.

Judith groped for her thread again. "So the clock is ticking for the would-be assassin. Luckily, Richard's condition means he's mostly away with the fairies, poor love. However, Terry convinced some high-flying doctors to put him on some experimental treatment. Psilocybin, a psychedelic drug found in magic mushrooms that has the promise to hold back the nightmares of neurological conditions. Research being done at the local university, which made sense to bring Richard down from Leeds and have him stay here."

"Of course," Terry said indignantly. "I was doing what anybody would do. Scrambling for solutions and help against a condition that was out of all our hands."

Judith nodded. "I know. It's a terrible condition. And to watch a loved one fade away before your eyes..." she fell silent for a moment, gazing into the floor before pulling herself together. "Awful. But for our killer, it was an opportunity. A way to do the old man over and avoid suspicions. And what better way of doing it but in front of a packed house of witnesses who would all witness the unfortunate accident."

DS Raymond Collins drew himself up to his full height and rounded on Terry, who was still sitting meekly on the sofa.

"So organising the party was the cover story, eh?"

Judith lay a restraining hand on Raymond's shoulder. "Easy, horsey. There are motives at play here. Nothing is straightforward and remember the rule: follow the money. The millions Richard had hidden in nest of shell companies. Money that was yours," she looked meaningfully at Terry. "But it wasn't a gift, was it? You had asked him to hide the money during your divorce." She winked at Linda. "Pay heed. Especially if he talks about a prenuptial."

"That's not true!" Terry said haughtily.

Judith cocked her head to the side and stared at him. "Really? Such an elaborate scheme of companies made it difficult to follow the money. Unlucky for you, I've had experience in such matters, as does the HMRC." She held up the printout Maggie had given her. "It's all here." She handed it to DS Collins. "And tax evasion is not as bad as murder, is it?"

"Avoidance, not evasion," Terry muttered in defeat.

"A drop in the ocean from everything you earn… except lately your unfiltered, controversial views have lost you a fair bit of income." Terry inhaled deeply but didn't respond. "And you had bought this fine place, which was a huge financial stretch, isn't it?"

Judith spun around to face Stephen. "Ah, Stephen. The young, jealous sibling. You never got on with your sister or brother, did you? Or your dad, for that matter. You always felt as if you were denied opportunity."

"After mother died, dad became a grouchy pain in the arse. And he wasn't much of a bundle of fun before that, either."

"Which is why you felt no remorse in trying to blackmail your brother."

Terry impulsively jumped to his feet. "What?"

"Your relationship with Miss Furches here would have perhaps reached a newspaper... do they still have them? Or an online gossip place, I suppose, to cough up a few grand. But to learn she was pregnant... well that's another matter for the gossip channels."

This time it was Rebecca's turn to remark. "You're pregnant?"

Linda Furches nodded shyly.

Judith pulled the three plastic pregnancy tests from her pocket and held them a lot. "All positive, and an odd thing to want to burn on a bonfire. That's what you were talking about when I overheard you that night. I thought it was Rebeca, but it was you two, worried about the news leaking. Especially as you're still married," Judith added, wagging her eyebrows salaciously. "To a rugby player. A big chap I believe."

"That's none of your business," Linda said.

Judith nodded. "I completely agree. I only bring it up because Stephen was planning to use it to extort money from his brother."

"This is pure fiction." Stephen took a stepped closer to Terry. "You said yourself, she's a mad old trout!"

Terry wasn't buying his deflection. He encouraged

Judith to continue. "How was he planning to do this, exactly?"

"With the help of Clive Wilson. The man whose career you had sabotaged. The man who vowed to do the same to you. During the wake, they were searching the house for evidence."

Terry's hands balled into fists, and for a moment, DS Collins thought he was going to get a glimpse of Terry Harman's notoriously short temper, but somehow he restrained himself.

"And that's not all I heard, was it? I heard that Terry had misplaced his phone, so he couldn't text Gary Mercer to start the display. Somebody had deliberately hidden it. More of that later." She circled a finger between Linda and Terry. "All of this brough Clive Wilson into the family fray. Except it didn't quite work out the way Stephen had intended." Judith turned back to Rebecca. "Did it?"

"What do you mean?"

"I don't suppose you were planning to fall in love with him, were you? But these things happen."

"I don't know what you mean."

"Of course you don't. It's almost as if I didn't see Clive tap-dance his way to your apartment near Baker Street. Or should I say, the flat belonging to the friend you mentioned? The one you'd arranged to start a new life once the tedious chore of looking after your father was over."

Rebecca went pale.

Judith pressed on. "So the stage was set. Stephen's little blackmail scam brought Clive into your life. You were surprised to find yourself falling in love with him and quickly picked up on the fact, Clive wanted much more than you Stephen was offering. It was his idea to speed your father on his journey, wasn't it? And along the way, try to change the will. He the one who persuaded you to get more psilocybin to make Richard even more confused? But where to get it? From the source would be best, so you set about making friends with an orderly linked to the university research lab."

"Gary Mercer," breathed Eastly as she put her cup down.

"Gary who you'd met while being treated for anxiety. A man who was quite smitten with you so could be easily manipulated."

Rebecca shook her head and took a threatening step towards Judith. "Nonsense. This is pure fantasy, backed up by what? You have no evidence!"

DC Eastly put her hand up. "But we have Gary Mercer's fingerprints on the tablet bottle you passed to me, Judith."

Judith gave a relieved chuckle. "When did you find that out? I was winging this part of the lecture!"

"They only came in as I was leaving the office."

"Forensics are terribly backed-up," added DS Collins who thought it best he was at least half aware of what was going on.

"Rebecca's prints were on it too," Eastly added. "But that would be expected as you were looking after him. But how would the DJ from the party get to them when you were all in the house at the time? He couldn't."

"I can't believe this..." Terry said. Despair had diluted his anger. He regarded Rebecca with puppy dog eyes.

Judith lay a comforting hand on his forearm. "Sorry, but it's true. You told me it was Rebecca who suggested the DJ. Strange that she would know a local one. But it was somebody she knew, and somebody whose equipment she could tamper with because he'd shown her how to use it." She regarded Rebecca sadly. "You got him to fall in love with you, so he'd do anything you asked. I knew that the moment he referred to you as 'Becs'." Rebecca folded her arms once more and looked as if she was going to burst. "And Stephen knew you'd fallen in love, because Clive was no longer going along with his plan, was he? Mr Wilson could see he had a bigger opportunity to cut your brother down and, through you, have more money than disgraced journalist could hope ever to earn. But being you, Stephen, you were not in full possession of the facts."

"What's that supposed to mean?" Stephen asked.

Judith smiled. "Exactly my point. A tad slow, dear. You argued with Clive on the phone as he was mucking up your scheme, so you eventually tried to frame your sister out of spite. That's why you lead me to the river where I found the pill bottle. It was a handy little dump Terry used to get rid of things people didn't want to see, so you tossed in the bottle, knowing it would get my interest."

Rebecca and Stephen eyed one another with a poisonous gaze.

Judith continued directing her thoughts to Rebecca. "But in reality, you had fallen for Clive Wilson, and *he* was manipulating *you*. You showed him Richard's accounts, didn't you? He was the one who worked out Terry was a tax evader–"

"Avoider," Terry added automatically.

Judith continued. "Which would make a juice addition to Terry's public disgrace. But the real *coup de grâce* came when you told Clive something Terry had entrusted to you. The reason that nobody can get proper bloody broadband in the village."

Most of the room swapped puzzled glances.

"Because the phone junction box keeps getting flooded. Terry wasn't stopping people trying to repair it. BT told me themselves that the land was waterlogged. A little more prodding around, and I learned the truth about your estate, Terry. It's unsellable. You'd been taken for a ride. The floodplain has extended almost up to the house. In a few more years, floods may very well soak this lovely carpet." She pulled a folded paper from her pocket. "Forgive me, I arrived a little earlier and had a little search through your bedroom. I found this surveyor's report."

Terry gave a grunt and nodded. "This place is worthless."

"Which is why you desperately need the money you'd given to your father. You're broke."

"That's right." It was a humble statement, for once devoid of any arrogance.

"And the problem there was your father had changed his will. While in the depths of his delirium, Rebecca and Clive had made him change the will so she would be the sole beneficiary."

"You bitch!" Stephen snapped at his sister.

"No!" Rebecca retorted.

Judith corrected her. "That's a big 'yes,' I'm afraid. But only after his passing did you become aware that he'd changed it *again* in a moment of clarity. Or rather, less confusion than usual. He'd bequeathed it all to his own sister, Gwen. Which was his original intention. She was the only one he regarded as having any family values. The only problem was that he'd amended that version of the will on his own, which meant that he'd made a mistake. He'd added Gwen as the first beneficiary, but Rebecca's name was still there. That meant if Gwen was out of the way, say, mysteriously poisoned, then Rebecca would suddenly revert to being the sole beneficiary."

DC Eastly chimed in. "The lab report confirmed traces of drugs on the sausage roll Judith took from the buffet."

"You tried to poison me?" Gwen screeched – lunging for Rebecca. Luckily, DS Collins pulled her away before her punch could land.

"Technically, she poisoned me," said Judith. "My gluttony saved you. They had mixed Richard's levodopa prescription with psilocybin, knowing that the levodopa can produce a fatal reaction with anybody who is on antidepressants."

Gwen was poleaxed in horror. Judith pressed on.

"I had to do a little research in that, and it's not the sort of thing you'd know, is it?" She looked questioningly at Rebecca. "It would need somebody with medical training to really know these things. And how to increase micro doses of psilocybin just enough to make an old man confused enough to walk out of a conveniently opened window."

"Mercer?" Collins asked, trying to keep up.

"Clive Wilson. Remember, he was a GP before he turned his hand to journalism. He'd be aware of the dangers."

Stephen frowned. "But Rebecca wasn't anywhere near you. I was watching her like a hawk during the wake because I wanted to find what she knew about the will. I was sure she knew something."

"Indeed, she did. Your mistake was inviting taking Clive Wilson over. He had laced the food, intending on killing Gwen. During the funeral, he was on the phone shouting at Gary Mercer to deliver more drugs just for that occasion." She glanced at DS Collins. "As his phone records will show."

She turned back to Stephen. "You were so desperate for this to work, postponing your trip to the States and all, that you were blind to their more nefarious activities. He was manipulating you just as much as your sister was. I bet he found what you were looking for in Rebecca's room and took it before you saw. It was a copy of Richard's will. One she'd made when she discovered Gwen's name had been added."

"This won't stand up in court," Rebecca spat. "I didn't kill daddy!"

"No. That precise distinction went to Clive Wilson. You drugged him up to the nines and sabotaged Gary Mercer's equipment in order to create a distraction. Clive was the one who had arrived, unseen by any of the guests, and gone up via the far staircase near the front door. He opened the door and positioned Richard next to it before the fireworks went off. Poor Richard was on a psychedelic trip when that happened, and Clive Wilson was gone while the rest of us clamoured around the body. He was the mastermind. You, his henchwoman. But equally culpable."

Rebecca's eyes flicked around the room as accusing gazes bored into her. Her eyes widened as she looked at DS Collins.

"You surely can't believe a word of this? Maybe it was Clive. But I didn't know about any of it! Where is your evidence? You have none because there is none."

"Not quite true," said Judith. "You see, love makes people do the darnedest things. Worse, are the depths a spurned lover will go to." She was taking delight in the increasingly puzzled expression on Rebecca's face. "Poor Gary Mercer. The way you manipulated him left him as the prime scapegoat should good old Detective Sergeant Collins get close, then you planned to leave him hanging out to dry."

DS Collins was slowly coming up to speed. "Which is how we discovered the copy of the will at his flat. He told me Wilson had been around to pay him for the drugs he'd delivered for the wake. They had an altercation, and Wilson left after hiding, rather badly, the will hoping it would incriminate him." Collins smiled, relieved that he had something to contribute towards his case.

Judith took back the lead. "He'd nicked some stock from work, but that was as far as his crimes went. When he discovered the situation between you and Clive... well, to say he was upset is an understatement. Devastated, more like. It left him in the perfect state of mind for a taste of revenge."

"Revenge?"

"The 'not wanting to take the wrap' sort."

Within seconds, Rebecca's posture transformed from defiant to startled cat. Any more extreme and she risked folding in on herself and blipping out of existence.

At that moment, Maggie made a perfectly timed entrance into the living room. She was talking to somebody trailing behind her.

"This way. She can't wait to tell you the good news herself." Maggie gestured toward Rebecca - and Clive Wilson bounded in like a love-struck schoolboy and embraced her.

"Oh, Rebecca! How I've heard the news..." he trailed off as he registered the crowd around them. They were not so alone after all. "What's going on?" He demanded angrily as his eyes locked with Terry Hardman.

"That's what I would like to know," Terry growled.

"Allow me," Judith said airily. "Mr Wilson here is under the impression the will reading was earlier this afternoon. He'd also been fed a few inaccuracies, such is the nature of today's fake news. First," she turned and held Gwen's hands tightly. "You passed away, after all. I'm afraid to say they got us both. Which of course means everything goes to you," she addressed the last to Rebecca. "Our unreliable narrator was Gary Mercer, who made the call from your phone." She directed that at Rebecca who suddenly patted her pockets for the misplaced item.

DC Sarah Eastly held it up and acted innocent. "Oh, this is yours? I found it earlier today when I came to inform your brother that we'd be attending the reading. Silly me."

If it were possible, Rebecca became even more terrified. Clive Wilson's face darkened.

"I don't know what's going on here, but this smells like entrapment!"

"That's not strictly a legal issue in the UK," DS Collins pointed out. "It's American, and I suspect you're thinking of that Sean Connery film."

Clive gripped Rebecca's arms tightly and pulled her closer. "Mercer told me he'd blackmailed you to part with some of the inheritance."

"And you came to save her," Judith said with a smile. "How very noble. Sadly, you were misinformed. But you came quickly fearing your part in attempting to poison dear Gwen would become public."

"That's–"

Judith quickly interjected. "Save your pleas of inno-cence. You coerced Rebecca into making Richard's condition worse. You both conspired to bump him off at the party." She stabbed an accusing finger at the journalist. "Remembering your GP days, you knew how to work the psilocybin just enough that a confused old man would walk out of an open window and scarpered out of the front before anybody saw you. I wager paying off the security guards to keep quiet, because they knew you were a journalist trying to rat out a story. A story you planned to engineer that would implicate Terry Hardman, a celebrity with a pregnant - still married partner - who is now on the verge of bankruptcy and tax evasion!"

"Avoidance." Terry chirped, this time without gusto.

Judith rampaged on. "Running his career, reviving yours, while you ride into the sunset with his now-wealthy sister!"

Clive Wilson gaped like a caught fish. He couldn't even summon the motivation to deny it. DC Eastly was still eating a biscuit with one hand and holding her coffee with the other.

"Sounds like a case to me," she said spitting crumbs.

Judith looked expectantly at DS Collins. He balled his fists a couple of times before stepping forward to confront the startled journalist.

"Mr Clive Wilson, I'm arresting you on suspicion of murder. And a few other bits and pieces, it seems."

Clive Wilson gaped in silence. Rebecca pushed him away and folded her arms, a scowl creasing her face. DS Collins was still trying to process events, and Judith's cock-sure smirk was distracting and irritating. He turned to Rebecca.

"And you too, Miss Hardman. You're both under arrest."

The weighty drama of the moment of spoilt by a gasp of glee from DC Eastly and a quick hand clap from Judith Spears herself.

# Chapter Thirty-Three

# $3^3$

The weather had brightened, and the deluge had turned Little Pickton an even richer hue of green, which pleased the Flower Brigade as they rushed out to resurrect their displays.

DS Raymond Collins drove his BMW slowly through the village, which had now reverted to its sleepy nature. Sarah Eastly sat in the passenger seat, her nose in her phone as she scrolled through emails.

"It was nice of Judith to give us that diagram," she said without looking up.

Collins grunted begrudgingly. The day after the initial arrests, Judith Spears had used two pieces of A4 paper to draw a flow diagram of events and motives and provided a checklist on each side to link the evidence. Collins had been affronted, not least because he had been struggling to iron out all the connections, but because Judith's paperwork was childish, simple, and exactly what he needed. She had been helpful to the point of annoying.

"Rebecca and Clive trying to screw Gwen out of her inheritance." Sarah shook her head.

"Well, strictly speaking, it was Terry's money."

"Speaking stricter it was mostly the taxman's."

"Now you're splitting hairs."

"Still. They almost got away with it..."

"If it wasn't for that pesky woman," Collins finished in a cod-American Scooby Doo inspired voice. He caught Eastly looking blankly at him. "Before your time."

Sarah put her phone down and looked earnestly at her boss.

"So it seems a shame to be doing this..."

Collins glanced at her but didn't reply for several seconds. He licked his lips.

"We can't have one law for one, another for... another."

"Eloquently put," Sarah said in a huff.

"You know what I mean."

The rest of the journey was conducted in cool silence. Judith Spears invited them into her cottage and made them a cup of tea as she was out of Nespresso capsules, and filled them in on subsequent conversations she'd had with Terry Hardman.

"So he won't be filing for bankruptcy?" Raymond said in surprise.

Judith shook her head. "With Clive Wilson on bail, he can't publish the story, so Terry's PR people have seized the narrative, as they say. Tax evasion stories are a gold mine for the famous. He reckons it will revitalise his career, like that comedian with the Lego hair, and the chap from that boy band. He's always on the BBC since he was exposed."

Sarah noisily stirred her tea. "Well, it just goes to show, doesn't it, *sir*?"

Raymond looked sidelong at her but didn't take the bait.

"Of course, there is little he can do about the land flooding, but it appears he has interest from a big American television company in doing a series about it." Judith raised her hands dramatically. "*Saved from the flood!*" she boomed in her best TV announcer voice. "An environmental series, of all things. That'll get him back on his feet. And with a baby on the way, I don't think he'll be fading in the shadows any time soon."

Sarah sighed. "It's poor Gwen who will get nothing. Not if HMRC has their way."

"She gained nothing, she lost nothing," Judith said pragmatically.

"She gained a more dysfunctional family and lost her brother," Raymond pointed out, then burned his lips on the piping hot tea.

"More milk, dear?" Judith asked.

"I had Stephen pegged for it," remarked Sarah, putting her cup down and reaching for the Bourbons Judith had arranged on a plate.

Judith poured her own tea and sat at the kitchen table. "He's condemned to go through life with a face that makes him look guilty. I don't blame him for developing a persecution complex. Maybe he'll have better luck in the States."

"He's not the sort to get away things," Raymond said levelly. "Unlike others."

Judith put down her cup and cocked her head at him.

"My dear detective. One would think you have matters on your mind. I should think you'd be basking in glory for cracking this case. And here's me, poisoned in the line of duty to prove Terry is innocent, only to find out he doesn't have a penny to pay me."

"For now," said Sarah.

Judith bobbed her head amicably. "Although I must confess, I have been the hero of the hour since the internet was restored. It turns out BT rerouted it all around Terry's estate, using cables on higher ground, so when it rains, we won't be disconnected. The village is delighted." She smiled pleasantly. "So, Raymond, you are off duty, aren't you? What's bothering you?"

Raymond Collins cleared his throat. "I am off duty, Judith, so Raymond is most acceptable. I'm off duty because of this." He took a folded piece of paper from his pocket and slid it across the table to Judith. She glanced at it, but kept her hands wrapped around her cup. Raymond leaned back in his seat. "Are you going to look?"

"Is there anything there I don't know?"

Raymond sighed. Her confidence was backbreaking to others. Or was it just him?

"There isn't much to discover about Judith Spears is there?"

"I keep myself to myself."

Raymond couldn't suppress a sarcastic laugh so loud that Sarah jumped in her seat.

"Sorry, I didn't realise you were a stand-up comedian, too." He tapped the folded paper. "That's about the sum total of Judith Spears' life. It's not much, because she died a long time ago. Aged sixteen. From tuberculosis."

Not a muscle on Judith's face gave away her thoughts. "That's a terrible shame," she said with heartfelt conviction.

"Only to reappear six years ago." He tapped the paper again. "How do you explain that?"

Judith puffed her cheeks as she mused. "I'm not terribly computer savvy. That's Maggie's department. But I suppose information gets easily lost these days. People sometimes fall between the seams." She shrugged. "Why, Raymond? How would you explain it?"

Raymond felt his cheeks burn. He leaned back in his seat, never taking his eyes off her. The silence was broken only by Sarah slurping her tea. Finally, Raymond spoke.

"You know, Judith, I don't think I can explain it." He looked sidelong at Sarah. "How about you?"

Sarah shrugged. "I suppose it's just one of those things." She reached for another biscuit. "And certainly it's one of those things we don't have time to look into. Especially with all that paperwork waiting for us."

"Oh yes, the paperwork." Raymond looked around the kitchen, then smiled. "I think you're right, Sarah. Judith has already given us one headache. Who needs another?"

He reached across and withdrew the folded paper, then he deliberately scrunched it up. Judith smiled and nodded in agreement.

"Precisely. And what a fine triumvirate we make."

Raymond chuckled and squeezed the bridge of his nose. "Please, no. That would be torture. Luckily, the odds of another crime happening way out here are diminishingly small."

Judith took a sip and gazed into the middle distance.

"Statistically speaking that is true. We can all relax for quieter times."

Amicable nods circled the kitchen table as a train whistle sounded in the far-distance and DS Raymond Collins reasoned that he wouldn't have much call to check in on Judith Spears in the future.

Almost none at all.

# Contents

| | |
|---|---|
| Chapter 1 | 1 |
| Chapter 2 | 3 |
| Chapter 3 | 12 |
| Chapter 4 | 16 |
| Chapter 5 | 21 |
| Chapter 6 | 29 |
| Chapter 7 | 35 |
| Chapter 8 | 42 |
| Chapter 9 | 50 |
| Chapter 10 | 57 |
| Chapter 11 | 62 |
| Chapter 12 | 70 |
| Chapter 13 | 78 |
| Chapter 14 | 84 |
| Chapter 15 | 94 |
| Chapter 16 | 100 |
| Chapter 17 | 107 |
| Chapter 18 | 113 |
| Chapter 19 | 120 |
| Chapter 20 | 126 |
| Chapter 21 | 133 |
| Chapter 22 | 140 |
| Chapter 23 | 149 |
| Chapter 24 | 155 |
| Chapter 25 | 161 |
| Chapter 26 | 169 |
| Chapter 27 | 175 |
| Chapter 28 | 184 |
| Chapter 29 | 193 |
| Chapter 30 | 202 |

Chapter 31                                      207
Chapter 32                                      212
Chapter 33                                      233

Also by Sam Oman                                243

*For my Family*

# Also by Sam Oman

DEATH ON THE LINE

(coming soon)

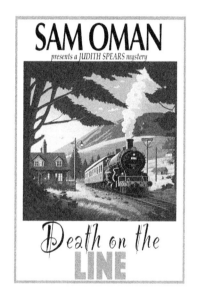

Printed in Great Britain
by Amazon